*Johnna turned to leave the
courtroom. That was when
she saw him.*

He sat in the back row, the only person left in
the room. Shock rocketed through Johnna as
her mind worked to accept his presence here in
Inferno, Arizona…here in this very courtroom.

"Hello, Johnna," he said, and stood.

Her first impulse was to run, to shove past
him and escape. The very sight of him, so
tall…so handsome, stirred old memories and
deep emotions.

"Hello, Jerrod…." Nice…civil…as if she were
speaking to anyone on the street.

But this isn't just anyone, her heart cried
out. This is Jerrod McCain, the man who
had once owned her heart…when she'd had
a heart to own.

Dear Reader,

The year is almost over, but the excitement continues here at Intimate Moments. Reader favorite Ruth Langan launches a new miniseries, THE LASSITER LAW, with *By Honor Bound*. Law enforcement is the Lassiter family legacy—and love is their future. Be there to see it all happen.

Our FIRSTBORN SONS continuity is almost at an end. This month's installment is *Born in Secret,* by Kylie Brant. Next month Alexandra Sellers finishes up this six-book series, which leads right into ROMANCING THE CROWN, our new twelve-book Intimate Moments continuity continuing the saga of the Montebellan royal family. THE PROTECTORS, by Beverly Barton, is one of our most popular ongoing miniseries, so don't miss this seasonal offering, *Jack's Christmas Mission.* Judith Duncan takes you back to the WIDE OPEN SPACES of Alberta, Canada, for *The Renegade and the Heiress,* a romantic wilderness adventure you won't soon forget. Finish up the month with *Once Forbidden...* by Carla Cassidy, the latest in her miniseries THE DELANEY HEIRS, and *That Kind of Girl,* the second novel by exciting new talent Kim McKade.

And in case you'd like a sneak preview of next month, our Christmas gifts to you include the above-mentioned conclusion to FIRSTBORN SONS, *Born Royal,* as well as *Brand-New Heartache,* award-winning Maggie Shayne's latest of THE OKLAHOMA ALL-GIRL BRANDS. See you then!

Yours,

Leslie J. Wainger
Executive Senior Editor

Please address questions and book requests to:
Silhouette Reader Service
U.S.: 3010 Walden Ave., P.O. Box 1325, Buffalo, NY 14269
Canadian: P.O. Box 609, Fort Erie, Ont. L2A 5X3

Once
Forbidden...
CARLA CASSIDY

Silhouette

INTIMATE MOMENTS™

Published by Silhouette Books

America's Publisher of Contemporary Romance

SILHOUETTE BOOKS

ISBN 0-373-27185-9

ONCE FORBIDDEN...

Visit Silhouette at www.eHarlequin.com

Printed in U.S.A.

Books by Carla Cassidy

CARLA CASSIDY

has written over thirty-five books for Silhouette. In 1995, she won Best Silhouette Romance, and in 1998, she won a Career Achievement Award for Best Innovative Series, both from *Romantic Times Magazine*.

Carla believes the only thing better than a good book to read is a good story to write. She's looking forward to writing many more and bringing hours of pleasure to readers.

Chapter 1

"Johnna Delaney, you are out of order!" Judge Orin Wellsby bellowed as he banged his gavel to emphasize his irritation.

"And you are a cantankerous old goat," Johnna muttered beneath her breath.

A white eyebrow rose and Judge Wellsby's pale-blue eyes narrowed. "You are coming dangerously close to a contempt charge, Counselor."

Johnna's client, Susan Boskow, a twenty-two-year-old mother of three charged with shoplifting, frowned, obviously worried by the heated exchange between the judge and her defender.

Johnna was aware of Chet Maxwell, the over-zealous, pompous prosecuting attorney grinning in smug delight.

She sighed and attempted to swallow her anger—

along with the bitter taste of her pride. "I apologize, Your Honor. I guess I just got carried away with the zest of defending my client."

Judge Wellsby, apparently mollified by her apology, banged his gavel once again. "Court is in recess until tomorrow afternoon at two o'clock."

As the judge disappeared from the bench, Johnna said goodbye to Susan, then began shoving paperwork into her briefcase.

"Are you all right?"

Johnna looked up at the familiar voice. Kelly Linstrom, who worked as her secretary and receptionist in her law office, eyed her worriedly.

Slapping another bundle of paperwork into her briefcase, Johnna drew a deep breath to steady her anger. "That old coot should have retired ten years ago," she exclaimed, her voice slightly unsteady. "He only sticks around so he can be a burr on my behind."

Kelly grinned impishly. "I'm not sure who is the burr on whose behind."

Johnna smiled tightly.

Kelly's grin widened. "Hopefully you can finish this trial without spending any time in jail for contempt. Don't you have your brother's wedding to attend tomorrow afternoon?"

"Yes, although from what Mark told me, it's just going to be a simple ceremony in the church down the street."

"I'd settle for a simple ceremony if only somebody would ask me to marry him," Kelly said ruefully. "I'll see you in the morning?"

"Bright and early," Johnna replied. As Kelly left the courtroom, Johnna snapped her briefcase closed, threw her empty coffee cup into a nearby trash bin, then turned to leave the courtroom. That was when she saw him.

He sat in the back row, the only person left in the room other than her. Shock riveted through Johnna as her mind worked to accept his presence here in Inferno, Arizona—here in this very courtroom.

"Hello, Johnna," he said, and stood.

Her first impulse was to run, to shove past him and escape. The very sight of him, so tall—so damnably handsome—stirred old memories and deep emotions, memories and emotions she had firmly repressed for the past nine years and certainly didn't want to remember or feel now.

"Hello, Jerrod." She was pleased at the controlled cool tone of her voice. "I didn't realize you were back in town." Nice, civil, as if she was speaking to anyone she knew.

But this isn't just anyone! her heart cried. This is Jerrod McCain, the man who had once owned her heart—when she'd had a heart to own.

He shrugged those impossibly broad shoulders, his blue gaze sweeping down her body, taking her in from head to toe. She felt his gaze as if it was the caress of his warm fingertips, and she stiffened defensively against the invisible assault. "I've been in town a little over a week. I've been staying out at my dad's place."

A week. He'd been in Inferno a whole week and she hadn't felt his presence, hadn't instinctively known he was near. Good. He was firmly and forever out of her life, out of her heart.

"Well, it's nice to see you," she said with what she thought was just the right touch of airy nonchalance. She headed for the door, but he stymied her escape by grabbing her arm.

"Johnna, wait. I need to talk to you."

She didn't want to talk to him. She didn't even want to look at him. She'd hoped he'd never return to Inferno, that she'd never, ever have to see him or talk to him again.

She pulled her arm out of his grasp. "It's been almost nine years, Jerrod. What on earth could you need to discuss with me?"

"Erin McCall."

The name exploded in Johnna's head—the name of the woman who'd stolen any hope for happiness that Johnna might once have had. The name sounded like blasphemy on his lips, and she flinched as if he'd physically hit her.

"I guess you've heard she was arrested two days ago for the murder of her husband?"

Johnna refused to meet his gaze. "I heard. But that has nothing to do with me." How could she not have heard? The whole town of Inferno had been buzzing with the news of Richard Kramer's murder.

She pushed past him and walked out of the courtroom and into the lobby of the courthouse, aware of him following close behind.

"She wants you to represent her."

Johnna whirled around to face him, her heart banging against her ribs. "That's absurd!" she exclaimed. "Why on earth would she want me?"

"She asked me to speak to you," he replied, not answering her question. He took a step closer to her, his blue eyes compelling her to acquiesce.

There had been a time when a single glance of those deep blue eyes with their thick dark lashes had been able to twist her inside out. But that had been another lifetime. They held no power over her now.

"You can tell her you spoke with me and my answer was no." For the third time she turned and walked away from him, exiting the building and walking out into the stifling heat and relentless sunshine.

To her surprise, he didn't follow. She walked to her car, got in, then drew a deep breath as the trauma of seeing him again fully infused her.

She'd thought she'd forgotten his irregular features, the thick dark hair and sensual lips, the nose with the small bump and his mesmerizing eyes. She'd tried to forget everything about him, but now her head was filled with the sum of him.

There had been a time when she would have driven a thousand miles just to catch his scent—that wildly masculine, clean fragrance that emanated from him. And there had been a time when she'd have done anything to taste his kiss, to know the heat of his mouth against hers.

There had been a time...a long time ago.

She started her car and pulled away from the curb, attempting to shove aside thoughts of him. Her hands trembled and her heart still beat an irregular rhythm.

She glanced at her wristwatch and realized if she hurried, she'd be able to make it to the ranch for dinner.

And after dinner she'd have to put in at least three hours of work—work that had nothing to do with her cases or chosen occupation, but rather work she'd been forced to endure by the terms of her father's will.

Bitterness swept through her as she thought of her father and his last will and testament. Adam Delaney had died almost three months ago, leaving behind a fortune in the form of a successful dude ranch.

Unfortunately he'd stipulated that all four of his children must work the ranch for a year, and only then would they be free to sell the place and split the profits. If they defaulted, the ranch went to Clara Delaney, Adam's spinster sister, whom none of the Delaney children could stand.

Johnna hadn't wanted anything to do with the ranch, but she'd agreed to abide by the terms of the will for her three brothers' sakes. Still, spending twenty-five hours a week working the ranch, in addition to her work as the only defense attorney in the small town of Inferno, was taxing her both physically and mentally.

And now Jerrod had entered the equation. He'd probably lied when he'd said he'd been back in town for a wcck. He'd probably heard about Erin's arrest and ridden back into town to her rescue.

Where had he been all these years? Was he married? With children?

Nine years was a long time, and yet for just a moment, when she'd first seen him, the years had faded away, leaving the taste of fresh betrayal and bitterness in her mouth.

She'd always thought that eventually they'd see each other again, couldn't believe that somebody who had been her world, somebody who had marked her life, her heart, in such a profound way, could just drift away, never to return.

In all her imaginings, she'd always been arrogantly smug about how well her life had turned out without him. She'd imagined him as a convict, a drunk, a man whose life had been filled with guilt and unhappiness.

But he hadn't looked wasted or dissipated. He'd looked vital and strong, successful and self-assured. She hated him for not looking like a man who had suffered.

Why on earth would Erin McCall—now Erin Kramer—ask her to represent her? Erin had to know that Johnna would not entertain fond feelings for her, that the betrayal in their past would forever stand between them.

As she turned into the entrance of the Delaney Dude Ranch, she once again consciously pushed aside thoughts of Erin...and Jerrod. They belonged in her past and she'd decided long ago that she'd never allow anything or anyone the power to hurt her again.

He'd blown it. He'd waited nine years to come back to Inferno, nine years to see Johnna again, and he'd totally blown it.

Jerrod McCain pulled into the trailer park where he had lived for the first twenty years of his life. And miserable years they had been, he thought as he pulled up in front of the double-wide trailer his father still called home.

He cut his engine, but remained in the car. Within minutes the exterior grew stuffy with the fiery end-of-day heat. Cracking open his window to allow in what little breeze there was, he stared at the trailer.

Few pleasant memories were associated with his time here. He knew there were trailer parks in other areas of the country where life was good and family values prevailed, where lawns were neatly tended and children's laughter rang in the air.

The Inferno Trailer Park was not such a place. Rather it had been, and continued to be, a den of iniquity, a dark place peopled with miserable souls, bad choices and the torment of hopelessness.

Reluctantly Jerrod left his car. Although he knew the interior of the trailer would smell of booze and stale cigarette smoke, he also knew the air conditioner would be a welcome relief from the heat.

"Ah, my saintly son has returned." Jerrod's father sat at the small burn-scarred kitchen table, a bottle of beer in front of him. From the look of his red-rimmed eyes and the slur of his words, it certainly wasn't his first drink of the day.

"Have you eaten today, Pop?"

"Not hungry." Mack McCain finished his beer and shoved the empty bottle aside. "Did you get all settled over at the church?"

Jerrod shrugged out of his suit jacket and grabbed a skillet from the cabinet. "Yeah, starting in two weeks, I'm ready to begin converting the sinners of Inferno every Sunday morning." He withdrew a stick of butter and a carton of eggs from the refrigerator.

Mack leaned back in his chair and rubbed a hand across his grizzled jaw. "Still can't believe it. My son—a preacher. Wonder what your ma would have made of it." He frowned and stood unsteadily. "Think I'll have me another beer."

"Why don't you have some eggs and toast with me, instead?"

Mack fell back into his chair. "I suppose I could eat a little."

Dinner was a silent affair, and once again Jerrod's thoughts returned to Johnna. Since coming back to town last week, he'd driven by her law office a dozen times, cruised by the small house where she lived just off Main Street, to catch a glimpse of her.

He should have spoken to her then—before Erin had been arrested, before he needed Johnna.

There had been a time when Johnna Delaney had been his lamp, the shining beacon that had pierced the darkness that was his life. He'd been nineteen and she'd been eighteen, and neither had been prepared for the passion, the wealth of emotion that had exploded between them.

He shoved the thoughts away, not wanting to remember the Johnna of his youth—so soft and warm, so sweetly giving. She'd been needy, and so had he. It had been a need greater than mere sex, stronger than loneliness. For a while they had assuaged that need with each other, and for a while it had been wonderful.

He cleaned up the dinner dishes, then realized his father had fallen asleep—or passed out—in his easy chair. Some things never change, Jerrod thought as he helped his father from the chair to the bedroom.

His father had been a drunk since the day Jerrod's mother had walked out on them. Jerrod had been seven, and he'd watched his father crawl into the bottom of a bottle and never crawl out.

He'd hoped things would change in the years he'd been gone. He'd written his father often, sent money on a regular basis and hoped the man would find the strength to build a life for himself. Instead, Mack had merely continued to mourn for a woman long gone and a love that hadn't lasted.

"You shouldn't have come back here, boy," Mack muttered as Jerrod covered him with the sheet.

"This place will suck the life from you. You should have stayed away."

Jerrod started to reply, then realized Mack had fallen back asleep. He left the bedroom, fixed himself a glass of iced tea, then stepped out the front door and into the simmering evening air.

The old wicker chair on the porch gave a familiar creak as he sank into it. He sipped his tea, his gaze focused on the trailer across the way. At one time it had been where Erin McCall and her mother had lived. During the time Jerrod had been away, Erin had surprised everyone. She'd finally made her way out of the trailer park by marrying Richard Kramer, one of the most affluent businessmen in town.

Jerrod had received a wedding announcement from Erin, along with a chatty letter telling him she'd finally found happiness. And now she was facing life in prison for the murder of her husband. What on earth had happened?

He took a long swallow of his tea and smiled as a dusty old Ford pulled up in front of the place. He set his glass down on the porch and stood as an old man climbed out of the car.

"Uncle Cyrus." He greeted the man with a warm embrace.

"I go away for a week and return to find my favorite nephew has finally come back home where he belongs."

Jerrod motioned to the wicker chair across from where he'd been sitting. "Want something to drink? Some tea or lemonade?"

Cyrus shook his head and eased himself down into the chair. "Nah, I'm fine. How you doing, boy? You look good."

"Thanks."

"You seen Johnna Delaney yet?"

Jerrod laughed dryly. "You never were one to waste time or mince words, Uncle Cyrus."

Cyrus McCain was the only person on earth who knew everything that had happened between Jerrod and Johnna so many years ago. It had been with Cyrus's help that Jerrod had left the trailer park, Inferno and Johnna behind.

"I'm seventy years old, boy. I don't have time to mince words."

Jerrod leaned back in his chair and picked up his tea. "Yeah, I've seen her." A vision of Johnna filled his mind.

For a moment he remembered her as he'd known her nine years ago. Then her hair had been long and thick and her eyes had been a soft ash-gray, which only hardened when she spoke of her father, Adam.

Today there had been no hint of softness about her. Her hair was almost boyishly short, and yet the style emphasized the sharp angles of her face, the fullness of her lower lip and the beauty of her eyes—eyes that no longer held any softness or vulnerability.

"She looks good," he finally said.

Cyrus nodded. "She's got that strong Delaney bone structure. I imagine she'll always be quite an attractive woman."

Jerrod frowned. "Have you heard about Erin?"

"I stopped in at the diner for some supper on my way back into town, and the whole place was buzzing with the news." Cyrus shook his head. "Somebody should have seen that marriage was a train wreck waiting to happen. Everyone in town knew Richard beat the hell out of Erin on a regular basis. I suppose she just decided to give it right back to him."

Jerrod took a sip of his now tepid tea. "She says she didn't kill him."

Cyrus raised a white eyebrow. "And I'm a fairy princess," he said.

Jerrod ignored him. "I asked Johnna to defend Erin today."

Cyrus stared at him in disbelief. "Tell me you're kidding."

"No, no kidding. Erin wants her."

"Did she tell you to kiss her—"

"She told me no," Jerrod said before Cyrus could finish.

"What did you expect her to say? You cheated on Johnna with Erin."

Jerrod's stomach knotted and a wave of guilt swept through him. Guilt that the years had done nothing to assuage. After years of soul-searching he'd thought he'd finally learned to forgive himself, but apparently it wasn't total absolution. "That was a long time ago."

"Matters of the heart don't know nothin' about time," Cyrus observed. "Your dad is a perfect ex-

ample of that. The wound is still as fresh today as
it was that Saturday morning when your ma left
him.''

"My father is a fool,'' Jerrod said with a touch
of harshness. "No woman is worth that kind of suffering.''

Cyrus said nothing. For a few moments the two
men simply sat in comfortable silence. As Jerrod
gazed at the man who was his father's older brother,
a burst of affection swept through him.

There had been many times when Jerrod had
wondered what might have become of him if not for
Cyrus's presence in his life. It had been Cyrus who
had listened to Jerrod's tales of woe as he'd been
growing up, Cyrus who had helped ease the absence
of his mother. And Cyrus who had, on the night
Jerrod had left Inferno, shoved a handful of money
and a Dallas address into his pocket and told him to
make something of himself.

And he had. Although the last thing he would
have believed when he'd left Inferno so long ago
was that he'd eventually become a minister, that was
exactly what he'd become.

"I'd better get on home,'' Cyrus said as he rose
from the chair. "I've spent the better part of the day
driving home from the cabin, and these old bones
are telling me it's time for a hot shower and my
bed.''

Jerrod stood, as well, and walked his uncle to his
car. Again the two men embraced. "Thanks, Uncle
Cyrus.''

"For what?"

Jerrod smiled. "For everything."

Cyrus waved his hands in dismissal of Jerrod's gratitude. "I'll see you tomorrow," he said as he climbed into the car.

A moment later Jerrod watched the old Ford disappear from sight. He returned to the porch, watching as the night shadows claimed the last of the sun.

Again his thoughts turned to Johnna.

He had betrayed her nine years ago and he'd lived every day of the time since regretting it. But she had betrayed him, too.

She'd allowed him to believe it didn't matter where he came from, that it didn't matter that she was a have and he was a have-not. She'd told him she loved him, but her parting words to him had revealed the truth.

He couldn't be certain of the forces that had brought him back to Inferno, but he steadfastly refused to believe one of those forces was any lingering feeling for Johnna Delaney.

The only thing he wanted from her was help for Erin. They had played at love once, but both of them had broken the rules. He didn't intend to play the game with her again.

Chapter 2

Johnna was running late. Susan Boskow's shoplifting trial had ended at five. The accused had received a sentence of probation and the promise that in the future if she found herself unable to feed her children, she'd reach out to the variety of agencies available for help.

Johnna's brother's wedding was set to take place at five, and she hurried from the courthouse, running down the street toward the tiny Methodist Church where Mark Delaney and his intended bride had chosen to be married.

"Sorry I'm late," she said as she flew into the small sanctuary where her brothers all stood, looking hopelessly ill at ease and out of place.

"You aren't late—the bride-to-be is," Luke said, a wicked gleam in his eyes. "She probably came to her senses and decided marrying Mark was a big mistake.''

Mark looked stricken and Matthew frowned irritably. "Knock it off, Luke," he said sternly. "Mark is nervous enough without your comments."

The beginnings of a headache banged above Johnna's right eye. "As usual, I see we're acting like one big happy family," she said irritably.

In the three months since their father's death, the four siblings had already faced an enormous hurdle. Mark had been attacked and a ranch worker had been killed in order to protect an illegal-alien smuggling ring that had been operating from the ranch.

The guilty had been arrested, including the family lawyer, who had been the executor of their father's will. A new lawyer had been retained, several ranch hands had been fired, and somehow in the middle of all the chaos, love had blossomed between Mark and April Cartwright, the woman who'd been hired as social director for the ranch.

The shared trauma had initially forged a fragile bond among the Delaney children as they united to fight an outside foe, but that bond was stretched thin as the need to unite passed and they were once again left to deal with one another without the tools necessary. They had not been taught how to interact with one another. A basic mistrust had been instilled in each of them, along with enough emotional baggage to last a lifetime.

God bless Adam Delaney. He'd been a shrewd businessman, one hell of a rancher, but he'd been a cold, mean-spirited man who'd taught his children nothing about love or family.

Mark looked as handsome as Johnna had ever seen him. He was clad in a black suit with a crisp white shirt. In fact, all her brothers looked exceptionally handsome without their trademark jeans and cowboy hats.

Mark eyed his watch worriedly, and at that moment April and her son, Brian, flew in. Mark's eyes flamed with an intensity so bright, so hot, Johnna felt the burn in the pit of her stomach.

Would a man ever look at her with such tenderness, such longing? A wistful yearning pierced her. Mark wore his love for April on his features—in the shine of his eyes and the curve of his lips.

Jerrod once looked at me that way. The thought snaked its way into her head and she shoved it away, knowing it was a false memory. She'd only *believed* that was the way Jerrod had looked at her. But it had all been a lie.

"I'm sorry I'm late," April said, looking lovely in a beige linen suit that emphasized her blond coloring. She smiled and took Mark's hands in hers. "Brian lost his dress shoes," she explained.

The eleven-year-old boy held out a foot, displaying his cowboy boots. "Those old shoes were too small, anyway. Besides, I told Mom you wouldn't care if I wore my boots."

Mark laughed, the worried lines that had creased his forehead gone. "I wouldn't have cared if you showed up barefoot," he said.

The church secretary stuck her head in the door that led to the small office. "Oh, good, I see you're all ready."

"All we need is the preacher man," Luke replied.

"He'll be right with you all," she replied.

Before anyone could say another word, the office door opened and Jerrod McCain stepped out wearing a black minister's robe.

For a moment Johnna thought this was some sort of dreadful joke. Seeing Jerrod in preacher robes was like seeing Santa Claus without his beard—it didn't fit.

She'd had no time to gather her defenses, to steel herself for the assault of seeing him again. She hadn't remembered his shoulders being quite so wide, his hair so rich and thick and his eyes such a piercing shade of blue.

She was suddenly aware of the run in her hose, the drab gray of her suit and the knowledge that her hair was probably standing on end.

As his gaze met hers, she raised her chin and refused to look away, hoping she conveyed a cool confidence and indifference that belied the tumultuous emotions racing inside her.

Finally he broke the gaze, moving to greet each of her brothers and the prospective bride. To Johnna's relief, the ceremony began almost immediately.

As Jerrod spoke the words that would bind her brother and April together as husband and wife,

Johnna tried to defend herself against the wave of memories that assailed her.

At one time she and Jerrod had talked of wedding vows and marriage. They'd spoken of forever and always, and for the very first time in Johnna's life, she'd felt valued...wanted.

It hadn't mattered that her father hated her, that he'd been bitterly disappointed that she hadn't been another son. It hadn't mattered that he had never forgiven her for surviving a difficult birth while his wife had died. None of it had mattered as long as Jerrod loved her.

Lies, she thought bitterly. All smoke and mirrors. No substance...no truth. Any love she might have entertained for Jerrod, despite the lies and betrayal, had died an irreversible death on the day she had buried Miranda.

She shoved these thoughts aside, refusing to go to the dark places in her soul where she mourned the baby girl she had lost. Although her brothers knew she'd lost a baby years ago, none of them had known the depth of her grief. She'd never shared that with anyone.

"I now pronounce you husband and wife," Jerrod said, his deep voice bringing Johnna firmly back to the present.

"And son," Brian quipped, his face beaming with happiness.

Mark laughed and ruffled Brian's hair. "And son," he agreed.

"You gonna kiss the bride, or do I get to do it for you?" Luke asked.

Mark gathered April into his arms. "I think, dear brother, this is a job I can handle all by myself."

As he kissed his new bride, Johnna was once again filled with a bittersweet wistfulness. She hardened herself against it, hating herself for entertaining any weakness or desire for anything remotely resembling love.

Fortunately, the congratulations were over quickly. Mark and April departed for a one-night stay at a bed-and-breakfast in town. Brian left with Matthew to return to the ranch, where he was spending the night with a friend.

Luke scurried out, probably in anticipation of a hot date, and Johnna headed for the door with him, unwilling to be left in the small church with Jerrod.

She needed time to think, and she headed to the place where she'd always done her best thinking. In the lobby of the courthouse, she stepped into the elevator and punched the button for the top floor.

When she reached that floor, she headed for the stairs that led up to the roof. She shoved open the door and stepped out, at the same time drawing in a deep breath of the hot arid air.

She walked over to the five-foot-high wall that surrounded the flat roof and peered out onto the streets of the small town.

The four-story courthouse was the tallest building in Inferno, and it was here on this very roof that fantasies had been spun and dreams had been dreamed.

There were many people who cursed the Inferno heat, but Johnna had always loved it. She shrugged out of her suit jacket, closed her eyes and allowed the hot air to embrace her.

Jerrod, a minister. How on earth had the man who she'd once believed had probably invented sin become a man of God? It simply didn't compute.

"I thought I might find you here."

She stiffened but didn't move, refused to turn around to face him.

"You always loved it up here."

She sensed his approach, knew when he stood just behind her, for his familiar, masculine fragrance seemed to wrap itself around her. "I still love it up here," she said. "I've always considered this my own little piece of the world, and at the moment I consider you a trespasser."

He was silent for a moment, then said, "I was once invited into your little piece of the world."

"That was a long time ago." She turned to face him. He'd shed his robe and now wore a pair of worn jeans and a white T-shirt that emphasized his bronzed skin and the sharp blue of his eyes.

"Yeah, it was a long time ago," he agreed easily, and moved to stand next to her.

For a long moment they stood side by side, staring out over the ledge. Although she didn't want to talk to him, she couldn't help the curiosity that surged up inside her. When he had left Inferno, where had he gone? What had prompted him to become a minister? How had he made it through college?

"I guess congratulations are in order," she finally said. "You've come a long way."

"For trailer trash, I've done all right."

Heat that had nothing to do with the outside temperature warmed her face as she remembered the hurtful words she'd flung at him the last time she'd seen him.

But she would not apologize. Instead, she sighed wearily. "Why did you follow me up here, Jerrod? What do you want from me?"

"Because I needed to talk to you, because I want you to reconsider your decision about Erin."

She looked at him once again. "I can't imagine why she would want me to represent her."

"I can tell you why." Again his gaze bore steadily into hers. "She told me if she can make you see she's innocent, then she feels like she can convince everyone. She also knows you aren't part of the good-old-boy network and that you're a true advocate for your clients."

"I'm glad she has such a fine opinion of me, but that doesn't change my mind."

"I would think that you'd jump at the opportunity to defend an innocent woman in a murder case. It's what you talked about years ago when we'd sit up here and talk about our futures."

But not Erin McCall. Her heart rebelled at the

thought. Anyone but Erin, she thought. "She can probably afford any lawyer in the state."

"She wants you." He paused a moment and raked a hand through his thick dark hair. The gesture was instantly familiar as she remembered he'd always done that when battling frustration. "Is this about what happened nine years ago? Johnna, please don't punish Erin for my mistakes."

She looked away from him, hoping he couldn't see how his words arrowed right to the heart of the matter. "Don't be ridiculous," she scoffed. "I got over what happened between us a long time ago." She looked back at him and asked dryly, "Did you really believe that somehow I'd spent the last nine years holding a grudge and mourning?"

"No, but I thought perhaps there might have been times when you thought of me. I know there were times when I thought of you."

His words seemed to burrow deep inside her and find the small place that held all her pain. Damn him. Damn him for coming back here.

"Look, I'll talk to Erin," she said. "Okay?" She just wanted Jerrod to leave, to go away and leave her alone. "I'll make an appointment and meet with her first thing tomorrow morning. Understand, I'm not making any promises. I'm just agreeing to talk to her."

"I appreciate it, Johnna."

"Good, then our business is concluded and I'd like some time alone, if you don't mind." She turned back to stare down into the streets.

She relaxed only when she heard his footsteps receding, then the soft closing of the door that led off the roof. She'd lied. She *had* held a grudge for the past nine years. She'd never completely gotten over Jerrod's betrayal.

She still mourned the loss of the dreams and fantasies they'd spun together in the blissful optimism of youth. There were moments in the long dark nights when she ached for the feel of his strong arms around her, his mouth pressed firmly to hers.

But she knew her loss had made her strong. Just like her painful childhood with her miserable father had made her strong. She neither wanted nor needed any man in her life. She was best alone...and alone was exactly how she intended to stay.

Jerrod might have forgiven himself for what he'd done to her years ago. God might have even forgiven him. But that didn't mean *she* intended to. There were some things that were simply unforgivable.

Jerrod sat in the tiny lobby area of the Inferno police station, waiting for Johnna to show up for her 9 a.m. appointment with Erin Kramer.

"Sure you don't want a cup of coffee?" Sheriff Jeffrey Broder asked from his desk in the corner.

"No, thanks, I'm fine," Jerrod replied. He shifted positions on the wooden chair, his thoughts drifting back to his conversation with Johnna the evening before.

For trailer trash, I've done all right. He winced

as he remembered saying the words. He'd sounded childish and petulant even to his own ears.

He'd believed he'd long ago worked through the baggage of that childhood label. But never had that name hurt more than when it had fallen from Johnna's lips so many years ago. They had been words that had destroyed his illusions of her, of his place in this town, but most of all, they had destroyed the illusions he had of himself.

But he was no longer the rebellious trash that had blown out of town with a chip on his shoulder and rage burning in his soul. He was now a man at peace.

He'd found his true vocation and had gotten a college degree. At the moment, however, more than anything he was a man who didn't want to see a dear childhood friend spend the rest of her life in prison for a crime he truly believed she wouldn't, couldn't commit.

He stood as Johnna swept in. He could tell by the narrowing of her eyes that she was not particularly happy to see him. Clad in a pair of tight jeans that emphasized her long, slender legs, and a biscuit-colored blouse that accentuated her dark hair and tanned face, she looked lovely, but tense.

"What are you doing here?" she asked with more than a little edge to her voice.

"I thought maybe I could help."

"I don't need help. I haven't even agreed to do anything other than speak to her." She nodded to Sheriff Broder. "Hi, Jeffrey."

"Johnna," he said as he rose from his desk. "Erin is our only prisoner at the moment, but I figured you'd be more comfortable in the conference room."

"Thanks, Jeffrey. The conference room will be fine." She looked back at Jerrod, her eyes an impenetrable smoke gray. "You're here. I suppose you might as well come on back with me." The invitation was not given graciously, but rather grudgingly.

Broder led them through the doors that led to the back of the police station and into a small conference room with a locked steel door. He opened the door and gestured them in. "I'll be right back with Erin," he said.

The door slammed shut behind him with a sickening thud that was all too familiar to Jerrod. He'd spent more than one night in the Inferno jail.

"I wonder what happened to old Sheriff Kiley?" he mused aloud.

"Last I heard, he'd retired to Florida and was spending his days playing golf." Johnna opened her briefcase on the table in the center of the room and pulled out a pad and pencil. "Why?" She looked up at him. "What made you think of him?"

Jerrod walked over to the table and sat in the chair next to where she would be sitting. "I was just remembering how often in my wicked youth I heard one of those steel doors slam shut behind me."

"Sheriff Kiley was just trying to keep you out of trouble by locking you up," Johnna said.

Jerrod nodded, knowing she was right. He'd never

been charged with anything, but occasionally he'd get in a foul mood, have a snoutful of beer and try to pick a fight. Kiley would keep him overnight until he'd sobered up or calmed down, then release him with a stern lecture.

The air in the tiny room was stuffy and, within seconds, filled with the scent of her. The scent of wildly blooming flowers with a hint of vanilla was the same fragrance she'd worn years before. To his surprise, it still had the power to stir him.

He stood and paced the room, amazed by how quickly he'd responded to her scent, and tried to dispel the memories that assaulted him. Memories of Johnna, warm and yielding in his arms. Johnna, eyes blazing flames of heat as she clung to him in breathless wonder.

Broder appeared at the door, Erin looking small and defenseless in front of him. He felt Johnna's shock when she saw the black eye and swollen lip Erin sported. "Just bang on the door when you're done," the sheriff said, then closed the door and left the three of them alone.

"Thank you for coming," Erin said to Johnna with as much dignity as possible in her current situation.

Johnna nodded and gestured the petite blond into a chair across from her at the table. "I hope Jerrod explained to you that I haven't agreed to represent you yet."

Johnna sat down as Erin did the same. As she began to ask background questions and make notes on the pad before her, Jerrod studied the two women who had played the most important roles in his life.

Erin—childhood friend, confidante and fellow dreamer. They had commiserated together, schemed together and, in one moment of sheer insanity, had effectively destroyed any hope Jerrod had of a future with Johnna.

He frowned and studied Johnna, seeing the changes the years had wrought. She was thinner than he remembered. And in his memories, her eyes had always been the soft gray of a predawn sky. As he had yesterday, he noticed no softness in those eyes now, rather a brittle hardness.

He wondered what life experiences had stolen the softness from her. He certainly wasn't egotistical enough to believe that it had been his long-ago betrayal. In the years since he'd been gone, surely she'd had other lovers. Funny how that thought bothered him more than just a little bit. He frowned and focused on the conversation.

"Erin, I haven't read any of the newspaper articles or listened to any news reports concerning your husband's murder. I'll need some background on your marriage...but let's start with what happened the night of the murder." Jerrod noticed that as Johnna spoke to Erin, she kept her gaze focused on the pad before her.

A muscle ticked just below Johnna's right eye, a sign of tension Jerrod recognized from the past.

Erin sat back in her chair, tears welling up in eyes

that looked as if they had already shed enough tears for a lifetime.

"It was Wednesday night. Richard had a business meeting and afterward he and some clients went out for a couple of drinks. By the time he got home around ten, he was drunk. And whenever he got drunk, he got mean." She swiped at her eyes, as if finding her tears more a nuisance than anything. "He'd slapped me around a hundred times before, but this time was worse than ever."

"Worse how?"

"Always before he'd been controlled with his beatings. He never hit me in the face and rarely where somebody might see bruises or cuts. But that night he was crazy."

"What set him off?" Johnna finally looked at Erin, the tic beneath Johnna's eye more pronounced.

"His navy-blue dress shirt." Erin stared at the tabletop. "I accidentally washed it with a white towel and it got white lint all over it. I'd set it on the dryer and was going to wash it again, but he saw it that night and went ballistic."

"He beat you often?" Johnna asked, and Jerrod realized the tic had vanished.

"He beat me whenever he drank. And Richard drank a lot."

"Are there police reports, hospital records, anything to chronicle the previous instances of abuse?"

"There are some hospital records, but we always lied to the doctors." She laughed bitterly. "You know, I stumbled down the stairs, I walked into a door…I was just clumsy and accident-prone. I don't know about police reports. Richard's best friend is…was Sam Clegg.''

"Deputy Clegg?'' Johnna's eyebrows rose.

Erin nodded. "When things got bad and I could manage it, I'd call Sam and he'd come over and calm Richard down, but I don't know if he ever made any reports. A couple of other deputies showed up a few times, but they always just talked to Richard.''

Johnna's pencil flew over the page of the legal pad as she scribbled note after note. Jerrod watched her intently, recognizing that, despite whatever reluctance she'd felt initially in meeting Erin, she was now completely caught up in the drama. She even seemed to have forgotten his presence.

Erin leaned forward and grabbed one of Johnna's hands. Johnna sat up stiffly, as if unaccustomed to any sort of physical contact.

"Johnna, I know we've never been friends, that there was a time you had reason to hate my guts. But I swear to you, that night, the night of the murder, Richard hit me so hard he knocked me unconscious, and when I came to, he was dead. Somebody had bashed his head in, but it wasn't me. I didn't kill him. I swear I didn't.'' She released Johnna's hand and again tears glimmered at her bruised and swollen eyes. "You've got to help me.''

Johnna stood and paced in front of the table. "Why me, Erin? Like you said, we've never been friends. Why would you want me to represent you?''

"Because Richard had powerful friends in this town, and I know you won't play any games. Because I think if you agree to take my case, you'll do everything in your ability to help me. I know you're honorable, Johnna, and I trust your integrity."

For a long moment Johnna stood staring at Erin, her forehead wrinkled with thought. She turned her head and gazed at Jerrod, and in the depths of her gray eyes, he saw a flash of vulnerability, a whisper of pain.

"Will you do it? Will you help me?" Erin asked softly. Johnna looked back at Erin, then nodded curtly and once again sat down across from her.

As the two women discussed the fee, Jerrod wondered why he had the strangest feeling that in helping one, the other might be healed.

Ridiculous, he scoffed inwardly. Erin needed help, but Johnna Delaney certainly didn't need to be healed. Still, he couldn't get that momentary flash of pain in her eyes out of his head.

In encouraging Johnna to represent Erin, he had either done a good thing or lit a fuse on a powder keg of emotions that might explode in all their faces. Only time would tell what the outcome would be.

Chapter 3

"How about some lunch?" Jerrod said as they left the jail.

Johnna looked at her watch in surprise. It was after eleven. She hadn't realized she'd been speaking with Erin for more than two hours.

Her first inclination was to reject his offer. She didn't want to have lunch with him. She didn't want to have anything to do with him. And yet, her pride alone didn't want him to think that she harbored any ill will toward him.

To let him know how deeply he'd hurt her all those years ago would give him power over her. And her pride wouldn't allow that. "Sure, lunch sounds good," she agreed.

"The diner?"

She nodded and they set off walking down the sidewalk. She'd been shocked to see him at the jail, hadn't anticipated he would want to be a participant in her interview with Erin. She should have known better. It was obvious he and Erin had maintained contact in the years Jerrod had been gone from Inferno.

"So what do you think?" he asked.

"You mean do I believe her?" Johnna thought about all the information she'd gained from Erin about the night of the murder. "I don't know... maybe. Although it really doesn't matter what I believe. It's what I can convince a jury to believe. I need to meet with Chet Maxwell before the arraignment Monday and see if there's a possibility he'll charge her with manslaughter rather than murder."

"She won't take a plea. She's innocent."

They ceased speaking until they were seated in a booth in the diner and had ordered lunch. Johnna's head spun as the realization of what she'd just agreed to sank in. She was going to defend Erin McCall—a woman she'd spent the last nine years resenting.

"Your brother and his new bride didn't plan much of a honeymoon," Jerrod said when the waitress had brought their drinks, then left. "Didn't I hear they were just spending one night at Rose's Bed-and-Breakfast?"

"That's right," Johnna said, then took a sip of her iced tea. "This is the busy season at the ranch and they've planned a more extended honeymoon when the ranch is dark in November.''

In the past ten years, the Delaney Dude Ranch had become a popular vacation place for tourists. It was open ten months out of twelve and closed for a month in the spring and another in late fall for maintenance and repairs.

''I was surprised to discover that Mark was the first of you all to get married,'' he said.

''Matthew might as well be married to the ranch. He'll probably never take a bride. Luke is so busy romancing everyone in the four-county area, he's a lost cause when it comes to monogamy and marriage.''

''And you?'' His blue eyes seemed to be searching inside her, seeking weaknesses—or secrets.

She met his gaze evenly. ''And I've decided I'm not cut out to be somebody's wife. I like living my life my way, without compromises or conditions. I'm set in my ways and perfectly happy alone. And what about you?'' she asked curiously. ''Do you have a wife tucked away somewhere? Perhaps a couple of kids?''

''No wife. No kids. I've been pretty focused on my ministry and that hasn't left much time for anything else.'' He leaned back against the red plastic booth. ''I have a lot of plans for the church, which I understand from Reverend Templeton is slowly dying from apathy. But eventually I'd like a wife and children.''

Was this the reason he was eager for Erin to be

acquitted? Perhaps he intended to take up where they had left off long ago.

It surprised her that the thought of the two of them together after all these years still possessed the power to hurt. She'd thought she'd become inured to the pain and knew she had to move past it in order to do the best possible job for Erin.

"When do you begin your work at the church?" she asked.

"Reverend Templeton is giving his farewell sermon tomorrow, and I'll take over starting next week." He paused a moment. "I was sorry to hear about your father's death."

She eyed him and said dryly, "Really. You were probably one of the few people who were sorry to see him go."

His gaze was so tender, she felt as if it reached inside her and stroked her heart. "Things never got better between you and your father?"

Johnna didn't reply as the waitress appeared with their orders. She placed Johnna's salad before her, then offered Jerrod a flirtatious smile along with his burger and fries. "Can I get you anything else?" she asked, and Johnna knew from the look in her eyes she was offering something to Jerrod that certainly wasn't on the menu.

"I think we're fine," Jerrod said, his gaze not leaving Johnna. The waitress pursed her lips in disappointment, then twirled and left.

"Isn't it some sort of sin for a woman to look at

a preacher like that?'' she asked with a burst of irritation.

Jerrod laughed, the deep rumble stirring the embers of memories Johnna thought dead. ''I'm a minister, Johnna, not a saint. And we were talking about you and your father,'' he said softly.

Johnna picked up her fork and stared at her salad. ''No,'' she countered, ''you were talking about my father.'' She set her fork down, her appetite buried beneath the weight of thoughts of her father.

''Nothing changed, Jerrod. From the time of my birth until his death, Father blamed me for killing my mother in childbirth and for not being born a son. He wanted a John, not a Johnna. I never could do anything right in his eyes.''

She didn't want to think about Adam Delaney. It was bad enough that he still controlled her from the grave, setting up ridiculous terms in his will that forced her to spend far too much time working on the dude ranch.

''I'm sorry, Johnna.'' He reached across the table and touched the back of her hand. His touch shot fire through her, and she jerked her hand away from his.

''Soon after you left Inferno, I did, too.''

He looked at her in surprise. ''You did? Where did you go?''

''I went to Phoenix, enrolled in college and lived in a tiny apartment off campus. I was there almost six years, but I came home regularly on breaks and holidays.'' She picked up her fork and speared a piece of lettuce, trying not the remember those first few months away from home, when she'd realized she was pregnant. "What about you? Where did you go when you left here?"

"Dallas. Uncle Cyrus gave me the name of one of his eccentric friends, and he was eccentric enough to believe I was worth investing money and tutelage." A smile curved his lips. "He was a preacher and took me under his wing and taught me about things I'd never known before."

"You mentioned that you were staying with your father. How's that going?" Johnna picked at her salad, not having regained much of an appetite.

Jerrod sighed. "Okay. Dad is still a mess, but I've finally come to the realization that I'm not responsible for saving him from himself. I'm looking for a house for us. I'd like to get him out of the trailer."

They fell silent as they each focused on their meals. As Johnna ate, she found her gaze drawn again and again to Jerrod.

As a young man, Jerrod had been handsome, but now, at twenty-nine, he had a quiet self-confidence, a strong maturity that had been absent years ago. And these traits transformed him from handsome to devastating. His finely honed features were more interesting now, with maturity and character reflecting within. His thick, dark hair invited feminine fingers to dance in the strands, and his sensual mouth looked as if it had been shaped just for kissing.

Even if he and Erin didn't work out, Jerrod would have no problem finding women interested in him.

The waitress was a perfect example of how Jerrod's attractiveness drew female interest. If it was his choice, he'd spend few nights alone in Inferno.

Suddenly Johnna needed to be away from here, away from Jerrod. The enormity of taking on a murder case, coupled with the past that she seemed to be having trouble keeping firmly in the past, made her need action.

She didn't want to be sitting here, studying the gorgeous features of the man she'd once loved with all her heart, a man who had absolutely no place in the safe, careful life she'd built for herself.

"I need to go," she said briskly, and shoved her barely eaten salad aside.

"But you've hardly touched your food," he protested.

"I'm not hungry. I suddenly realize I've got a lot to do. I've got to talk to Chet, gather reports and plan a defense strategy."

"You're going to need help."

She nodded, having already thought of that. "I've got a friend in Phoenix, a lawyer friend who I'm hoping will come out here to help."

He touched her again, his warm hand reaching out to cover hers. This time she fought the impulse to pull away. "I'm not a lawyer, but I want to help in any way I can."

He removed his hand from hers and Johnna stood. "I'm sure Erin appreciates your support." She opened her purse to get money for her meal.

"It's on me," he said.

"Thank you," she said, and closed her purse. She murmured a quick goodbye, then left the diner, hoping the heat of the midday sun would burn away the feel of his hand on hers.

Fifteen minutes later she was ushered into Chet Maxwell's office, where the chubby prosecutor greeted her with a big grin. "I hear we're going head-to-head on the Kramer murder case."

Johnna raised an eyebrow in surprise. "News travels fast."

He laughed and gestured her into the chair in front of his desk. "This is Inferno. The minute you walked into the jail this morning, half-a-dozen people began talking."

"I don't know why we bother publishing a newspaper every morning," Johnna said wryly.

"So." Chet sat behind his desk and reared back in the oversize chair. "I assume that's why you're here—the Kramer case."

For the next hour Johnna argued, cursed and conceded points of law with Chet. She came away from the meeting knowing that Erin would be charged with first-degree murder and that Chet intended to ask the judge for no bail.

He promised to have his secretary personally deliver copies of all pertinent paperwork to her office in the next couple of hours.

Johnna left his office and walked the three blocks to her own law office. She unlocked the door and entered the small office that comprised two rooms—the reception/lobby area and her private office. Her receptionist worked on a part-time basis and didn't work on Saturdays.

Johnna headed to the private office and sat down behind her desk, her thoughts tumbling turbulently in her head. Her father had never seen her office. He'd never shown any interest in the fact that she'd passed the bar, leased an office or begun a practice. But then, he'd never shown any interest in her other than to tell her how utterly worthless she was.

In retrospect, Johnna realized her relationship with Jerrod had begun as a rebellion and it had been the first time she'd achieved her goal, resulting in her finally gaining her father's attention. They'd had the biggest row of their lives over her seeing Jerrod.

But it hadn't taken long for rebellion to become something deeper, more profound, and the love she'd felt for Jerrod had been the first good thing in her life.

And then he'd destroyed it.

Funny, most of her anger had never been directed at Erin. Erin hadn't broken promises, destroyed faith or betrayed trust by sleeping with Jerrod. No, Jerrod had done all those things by sleeping with Erin.

Pain ripped through her as she remembered the night of his confession. She'd waited for him as usual at the end of the lane leading to her family ranch, her heart singing with the knowledge that soon she'd be in his arms. But when he'd arrived, he hadn't taken her in his arms; instead, he'd told her that the night before he'd had sex with Erin. And that was the night Johnna's world crashed down around her.

She'd been so sure he'd deny it, that he'd tell her he'd never so much as kissed Erin McCall. But he hadn't denied it, and the memory of that moment of truth still had the power to make her ache inside.

Shoving aside those thoughts, she picked up the telephone and dialed the long-distance number that would connect her to Harriet Smith. She didn't want to think any more about Jerrod McCain. She had to focus on Erin's case.

She was grateful to hear the raspy deep voice that picked up on the second ring. "Harry, it's me."

"Johnna! What a pleasure to hear your voice."

"And yours," Johnna replied, warmth flooding through her as she thought of the older lawyer who had played an integral role in Johnna's pursuit of a law degree. Without Harriet's support and friendship during the grueling years of law school, Johnna might have given up.

"What's up?" Harriet asked.

"I need your help. How would you like to second-chair a murder trial?"

"Tell me where and when and I'm there."

Johnna smiled. "Here and yesterday." For the next few minutes the two women finalized things, then hung up.

It would be good to see Harriet again, although she'd refused to consider being a houseguest of Johnna's and instead, had asked Johnna to get her a room at the local bed-and-breakfast.

Ninety minutes later Chet Maxwell's secretary knocked on the door of the office and handed Johnna a manila envelope. Johnna thanked her, then went back to her desk and began reading and making notes.

She didn't realize how long she'd been working until she stopped to stretch and realized the room was growing dark with the approach of night.

Checking her watch, she was shocked to see it was almost nine. She'd worked through dinner and the lonely evening hours. Now night shadows deepened to possess the tiny town and Johnna was exhausted.

Her exhaustion was physical. Her shoulders ached and her back was sore from sitting for so many hours. But her mind whirled with all the information the reports had contained.

Sheriff Broder and a couple of his deputies had responded to a disturbance call and had arrived at the Kramer home at eleven-thirteen Thursday night. Erin answered the door, dazed and obviously beaten and led them into the living room where Richard Kramer lay sprawled on the floor, dead from several blows to the back of the head. Nothing had been found at the scene that appeared to be the object used to hit the victim.

The report had described Erin as "nearly incoherent" and "hysterical." The statement she had given the sheriff later that night was the same as what she'd told Johnna.

Johnna packed the files and reports into her briefcase, then shut off the office light and locked the place up tight for the night.

Although she only lived a few blocks from her office, she'd driven her car that morning because she'd intended to drive out to the ranch and put in a couple of hours work there. But now it was too late to go to the ranch.

Main Street had shut down for the night and the street was deserted. Inferno wasn't the place to live if you liked nightlife. There was only one bar, at the edge of town, that remained open after 8:30 p.m. The rest of the town folded up at that time.

She approached her car and frowned as she saw that something appeared to be smeared across the dark blue paint of the hood. As she walked closer she realized it was white spray paint.

''Terrific,'' she muttered. Apparently some of the bored youth of Inferno had run amuck. Then she spied the note tucked beneath her windshield wiper.

She plucked out the note and opened it.

DROP THE KRAMER CASE OR DIE.

The words were handwritten in block letters, and Johnna stared at them for a long moment as a shiver of apprehension crawled up her spine. She tucked the note into her purse, then drove her damaged car down the street to the police station. As she drove, she contemplated exactly what the note meant.

Perhaps somebody thought Erin was guilty as hell and resented the fact that anyone intended to defend her. This possibility determined that whoever had painted her car and written the note was probably a moron who didn't understand the way the judicial system worked and didn't realize that somebody would defend Erin no matter what.

Or her initial reaction might have been right— kids out for a night of mischief who'd heard she was Erin's lawyer. In either case, whoever was responsible apparently didn't know Johnna very well. They certainly didn't realize that when she was pushed, she didn't quit. She pushed back.

It had become habit for Jerrod, after tucking his father into bed, to pour himself a glass of iced tea and sit out on the porch and relax as the night shadows cooled the day's heat.

After he'd left the diner earlier in the day, he'd met with Shirley Swabb, a real-estate agent, and she'd taken him to see several houses that were for sale in town.

The trailer park was dying, was for all intents and purposes dead. There had once been no less than twenty trailers in the area, but now there were only twelve, and three of those were abandoned and now were just ugly tin skeletons awaiting an official burial.

However, it wasn't the demise of the trailer park that encouraged Jerrod to look for a new home for his father and himself, rather it was the need to remove his father from the haunting memories of his wife.

Jerrod's mother had lived in the trailer for eight years before she'd left to buy the proverbial "pack of smokes" and never returned. That had been nearly twenty-three years ago, and still, at least for Jerrod's father, her spirit lived in every room.

Jerrod sipped his tea and tried to remember the woman who'd given birth to him. He had very few memories of her, and his strongest were of a woman who'd been miserably unhappy.

He thought of his father. How horrendous it must be to be tormented by thoughts of a lost love for twenty-three long years. And yet, hadn't Jerrod himself been tormented by thoughts of Johnna for the past nine years?

He rejected this momentary illumination. Ridiculous, he scoffed. He'd gotten over Johnna Delaney long ago. The fact that he'd had no real relationship with a woman since her had nothing to do with anything other than he'd chosen a lifestyle and embraced a set of moral standards for himself that didn't allow for passionate, uncommitted relationships.

Still, when he'd felt her hand, small and soft beneath his at lunch earlier in the day, he'd wondered if the magic that had once sparkled between them might still exist, or if it had been forever extinguished beneath the weight of betrayal and the poison of cutting words.

A car approached, its beams slicing through the darkness and momentarily blinding him. It parked in front of the trailer, and he stood, surprised to see the woman who had been on his mind.

He set his glass down and left the porch to greet her. "Johnna," he said, wondering what on earth had brought her here.

"Thought you might like to see the new paint job somebody did on my car." She gestured to the hood.

Jerrod moved around to the front of the car to get a better look. "When did this happen?"

"I'm not sure. Sometime this evening while I was in my office and the car was parked out on the street."

"Did you report it?" he asked, trying not to notice how the moonlight brought out the rich luster of her hair and gave her features a soft, silvery glow.

She leaned against the side of the car. "Yeah, but I'm sure nothing will come of it." She dug in her back pocket and handed him a folded piece of paper.

"What's this?"

"A note that was stuck under my windshield."

He tried to make out the words in the darkness, but couldn't. "Come on up to the porch," he said.

Together they walked to the tiny porch and he read the note, then looked at her sharply. "You showed this to Sheriff Broder?"

She nodded and sank into one of the wicker chairs.

"Want some iced tea? A soda?"

"Tea would be wonderful," she replied.

Jerrod grabbed his empty glass, then went inside to get the drinks. For a moment he leaned against the counter and fought a wave of anger as he thought of anyone threatening Johnna. The anger was tempered with a sickening swirl of fear for her safety. He checked on his father, who was sleeping soundly, fixed two glasses of tea, then stepped back out to the porch and handed her one.

"Thanks," she murmured, and took a sip.

In the yellow glare of the porch light, he noted she looked drawn. He sat in the other chair and looked at her intently. "Maybe you should drop the case. I can give Erin the names of several good attorneys in Texas. They'd be glad to take her on."

She eyed him with disbelief and he saw the stubborn thrust of her chin. "You really think I'm going to allow an anonymous note and a little spray paint to scare me away? Not a chance."

"I should have known better," he said dryly. There were times he'd wondered if his appeal to her had been based on her stubbornness and her refusal to bend to what others thought appropriate.

"What I can't understand is why somebody would care whether I defend Erin or not." She frowned thoughtfully. "It's not like if I don't do it, nobody will."

"Maybe somebody is afraid that you're such a good attorney you'll get Erin off."

She emitted a burst of laughter. "Boy, can I tell you're new in town." She frowned again. "My law office has only been open less than a year. I haven't exactly made a reputation yet."

"You're wrong." He pulled his chair closer, so

close his knees bumped hers. "You have made a reputation for yourself as a determined and passionate advocate for the downtrodden in this town. You're a good lawyer, Johnna, just as I always knew you would be."

Her eyes flared with a momentary glitter of gratitude, as if she rarely heard words singing her praises. She'd been a teenager who'd needed to be told often that she was good and worthwhile, and it appeared that much hadn't changed in the intervening years.

And something else that hadn't changed. When they'd been young and in love, Jerrod had been fascinated by Johnna's mouth. He'd seen her full, bottom lip as a blatant invitation and now found himself remembering the sheer pleasure of kissing her.

Johnna kissed like she did everything, throwing herself into it with passion and heart. A spark ignited in Jerrod as he thought of the kisses they'd shared in the past. Hot, fiery kisses that had stirred him to his core. Heaven help him, but she was a temptation.

"Jerrod, you're staring," she said with a trace of embarrassment.

"Sorry." He mentally shook himself and sat up straighter in his chair. "So, where do you go from here with the case?"

"The first thing I intend to do is hire Judd Stevens to do some investigative work for me. I want to get as much background material as I can, and with having to work twenty-five hours a week at the ranch, I just can't do it all myself."

"Why do you have to work twenty-five hours a week at the ranch?"

Again a frown creased the smooth skin of her forehead. "My father's will." She paused a moment to take a sip of her tea, the tip of her tongue darting out to lick her lips. Again Jerrod felt a burst of heat suffuse him. "It's my father's attempt to control us beyond the grave."

"What do you mean?" Jerrod took a long swallow of his own tea in an effort to cool himself.

"According to Father's will, none of us can inherit the ranch for a year, and during that year we all have to work twenty-five hours a week there. Otherwise we forfeit everything and Aunt Clara gets it all."

"Why would he do something like that?"

She stood, as if unable to discuss her father from a relaxed position. "Because he was a mean, hateful man who loved to control the four of us." She paced in front of Jerrod. "I wouldn't mind forfeiting myself. I've always hated the ranch."

Jerrod said nothing, although he knew better. "But," she continued, "the ranch is so important to Matthew. I have my law practice, Luke has his music and Mark now has April. Matthew has nothing but the ranch. I can't be the one to take away his dream."

"So the will is set up so that if one of you defaults, you all lose?" Jerrod asked, and got to his feet, also.

Her fragrance surrounded him, the scent of summer flowers and vanilla, and he stepped closer to her, drawn to her as he had been so long ago.

Was the magic they'd once had gone forever? Never to be recaptured? Crushed beneath the weight of his youthful mistake and the circumstances that had brought them here in this place in time?

She nodded absently in answer to his question. "I've got to get home. I have a full day planned for tomorrow. I need to talk to people who knew Erin and Richard." She stepped off the porch and he followed her.

When she reached her car, she started to climb in, but he stopped her by touching her arm. She looked up at him, her strong, beautiful features painted by the moonlight.

"Johnna, I want you to take this threat seriously." He nodded to indicate the paint on her hood.

"I'm sure it's nothing more than the work of a moron," she said.

"Even morons can be dangerous." He wanted to kiss her. He wanted to capture those lips with his, feel the heat of her body pressed against his, recapture the magic that had become lost.

Unable to help himself, he reached up and touched a finger to her cheek. She flinched away from him, her gaze hardening, and got into her car. "I'll be careful," she said, and started the engine.

As she pulled away, Jerrod shoved his hands into his jeans pockets and watched until her taillights had disappeared from view.

Chapter 4

A smile curved Johnna's lips as she drove down Main Street toward her house. She'd had a productive morning. She'd met with Judd Stevens, the private investigator, and had arranged for him to begin work for her.

After meeting Judd, she'd picked up Harriet Smith, her good friend and fellow attorney, from the tiny Inferno airport and had just left the older woman at the bed-and-breakfast where she would be staying for the duration of Erin's trial.

It was terrific to have Harriet here, not only helping her with the legal machinations of her first murder trial, but also as emotional support. Only Harriet knew the full depth of Johnna's despair when she'd lost Jerrod, then when she'd lost her baby girl. Only

Harriet understood the grief that would always reside in a portion of Johnna's heart.

Turning from Main onto Oak, her gaze shot to the house third from the corner. It was a charming little two-story, with gingerbread trim and a long front porch. More than that, it was Johnna's safe haven, her private space—her home.

Here was the one place she felt as if she truly belonged. She'd picked the house and its furnishings with great care, creating a nest where she fully anticipated living the rest of her life. Alone.

She'd decided to come here, grab a bite of late lunch, then head to the ranch and put in a couple of hours of work there. Harriet had insisted she needed the day to acclimate herself to the small town and had further insisted Johnna leave her to her own devices for the day. They would meet first thing in the morning for Erin's arraignment.

As Johnna got out of her car, two people standing in the front yard of the house across the street caught her attention. A wave of dismay swept through her as she recognized Jerrod and Shirley Swabb, the local real-estate agent.

That particular house had stood empty and been for sale for some time. Surely Jerrod wasn't considering buying the place. But what else could he be doing there with Shirley?

It was bad enough Johnna had to share this small town with Jerrod, bad enough he apparently intended to be a big part of Erin's support. Johnna certainly did not want to share this street with him.

She didn't want to have to look out her window and see him day in and day out.

"Hi, Johnna." Shirley waved, her broad face beaming as Johnna approached.

"Hi, Shirley, Jerrod." Johnna tried not to notice how handsome Jerrod looked. He was clad in a pair of charcoal slacks and a white shirt, the sleeves rolled up to expose well-developed forearms sprinkled with dark, curly hair.

His eyes were the color of the sky overhead, a blue so intense it almost hurt to look at them. There had been a time when Johnna had been able to lose herself in those blue depths.

"What are you doing here?" she asked him.

"Looks like we're going to be neighbors," Jerrod replied.

"Jerrod is buying the place," Shirley added with another of her big, salesperson smiles.

"Why? It's a wreck." Shirley's smile slid away beneath Johnna's pronouncement. "The porch is sagging, one of the windows is broken. It needs painting."

"All cosmetic," Shirley replied stiffly, and shot Johnna a glare.

Johnna ignored her. "Jerrod, surely you can find a place that doesn't need so much work." Someplace not on my street, someplace on the other side of town, she wanted to scream.

"I like this house," Jerrod replied, his gaze unreadable as it lingered on her. "Besides, Shirley is right. It's structurally sound. It just needs a little tender, loving care. In fact, Shirley tells me your brother does a lot of carpentry work.''

''I'm sure Luke is far too busy to take on another project,'' Johnna replied. She knew she sounded churlish and petulant, and she hated herself for it. But he was stirring old emotions, emotions she found more and more difficult to shove away.

''My father needs a project and this place will be just the thing for him,'' Jerrod said.

''We're on the way to my office to sign the paperwork,'' Shirley added coolly, obviously irritated by Johnna's attempt to interfere in a sale.

''I promise you I'll be a good neighbor,'' Jerrod said, a knowing smile curving his lips.

''I'm sure you will be.'' Johnna felt the heat of a blush warm her face and wondered how transparent she had been.

''How was church this morning?'' she asked grudgingly.

''Wonderful. The good reverend delivered a beautifully moving goodbye sermon. Unfortunately there was only a handful of people there.''

''I'm sure you'll turn that around in no time,'' she said, then added, ''And I hope you and your father will be very happy here.'' She realized she was fighting a losing battle with the house and refused to give him the satisfaction of hearing any more of her protests.

Before anyone could say anything else, she spun on her heel and strode back to her house.

Once inside, she dropped her briefcase by the

front door, then stood at the front window and stared outside. She watched as Jerrod took the For Sale sign down and walked it over to lean it against the side of the garage.

When he'd touched her face the night before, she'd wanted to fall into his arms, feel the heat of his mouth, allow him to take whatever he wanted or needed from her. And that had frightened her.

At eighteen she had been positively besotted with Jerrod McCain. She'd given him power over her mind, her body and her heart. And he had thrown it all away, leaving her in a state of devastation she'd never fully recovered from and never again wanted to experience.

As Jerrod climbed into Shirley's car, Johnna turned away from the window. She didn't want to think anymore about Jerrod McCain. He was a part of her past—a past that had shaped and formed the strong, independent woman she'd become.

For the next hour Johnna was on the phone. She set up a meeting with Sam Clegg, the deputy who had responded to Erin's emergency call on the night of the murder, then called the Inferno hospital to request all records pertaining to any emergency visits Erin had made during the past several years.

Finished with her calls and with lunch, she headed out to the family dude ranch to do some of the hours required of her for the week.

As she drove, a familiar ball of anxiety formed in her chest. She had no good memories of her childhood home. The ranch represented only misery to her. If not for her brothers, Johnna would have walked away from the terms of her father's will and allowed the entire place to go to her crazy aunt Clara.

The guest book must be full, she thought as she pulled into her usual parking place. People were everywhere, despite the intense early-afternoon heat. She spied her brother, Luke, hammering on a portion of corral fencing. She parked her car, got out and headed toward him.

Adam Delaney had been an intensely handsome man, and he'd passed his handsome features to his sons. Luke's dark hair was longer and curlier than his brothers, but he had the Delaney dark coloring and strong features.

"Hey, sis." He greeted her with one of the wicked, sexy grins that made him legendary among the women, both young and old, of Inferno. "Come to spend a little court-enforced time with your beloved family?" He swiped a hand across his sweaty forehead and leaned against a fence post.

"Something like that," she replied. "Looks like we've got a full house."

He nodded. "We're booked solid for the rest of the year. But I hear you're going to be pretty busy with a new client."

Johnna smiled ruefully. "There are never any secrets in Inferno, are there."

"A murder is a pretty big secret for any town to try to keep," Luke said.

"Are you keeping pretty busy?" Johnna asked.

"Sure, besides working here, Iva May Caldwell has me building a new deck, and then there's my nights at the Honky Tonk."

The Honky Tonk was a bar at the edge of town where Luke spent most evenings playing guitar, singing and, as far as Johnna was concerned, drinking far too much.

"So I'm sure you're too busy to take on another project," she said. Even though she knew it was irrational, she didn't want Luke working on Jerrod's new house. Perhaps if Luke was unavailable, Jerrod would buy a place that didn't need so much work— a place far away from Johnna's home.

Luke gazed at her with a wry grin. "I don't know exactly why you're dancing around it, but I've already told Jerrod I'd help him."

Dismay swept through Johnna. "Maybe you could change your mind?"

Luke hitched the hammer through his belt loop and stared at his sister. "What's going on, Johnna? It's not like you to play games. You still holding a grudge against the new minister in town?"

"Of course not," Johnna replied instantly. The last thing she wanted was anybody to think Jerrod still had the power to affect her in any way. "I got over Jerrod McCain a long time ago."

"That's what I thought," Luke replied. "But now I'm not so sure."

Johnna sighed. "Trust me, there is absolutely nothing between Jerrod and me, and it's going to stay that way. I'd better get inside and get to work."

She was more irritated with herself than anything as she walked back to the large ranch house. She was being ridiculous. What possible difference did it make if Jerrod lived across the street from her? She was an adult, and in control of her emotions and her future. And there was certainly no place in either for Jerrod McCain.

None of her brothers knew that Jerrod had been the father of her baby. She'd been vague about the timing of the loss of Miranda, implying that she'd gotten pregnant in Phoenix. And her brothers, in true Delaney fashion, hadn't pushed for details.

Johnna's work at the dude ranch was a mixed bag. She spent the time she was there answering the phone and confirming reservations, but also worked on a variety of publicity projects in an attempt to continue the success and reputation of the ranch as a vacation fun spot.

She'd worked at her desk in the office for almost two hours when her eldest brother, Matthew, walked in, his forehead lined with tension.

"What's up?" she asked, instantly on guard. There were times Matthew reminded her so much of their father, and never more so than when he frowned.

Where Luke looked like a sexy bad boy, and Mark had the clean-cut look and the friendly smile of the guy next door, Matthew was like a stern, forbidding father figure.

"Would you please explain to me why on earth

you decided to get involved in the Kramer murder case?''

Warmth suffused Johnna, and her automatic response was rebellion against the arrogant coldness in his voice. ''Sure. I knew it would irritate you.''

Matthew didn't dignify her response with one of his own. Instead, he propped a hip on the edge of her desk and raked a hand through his hair. ''Johnna, this isn't a case you should take. It's a loser. Everyone knows Erin killed him.''

''Gee, I wonder why we're even bothering with a trial,'' she said. ''Let's just lock her up and throw away the key, and to heck with due process and constitutional rights.''

''I'm not arguing the fact that she deserves a defense. But why does it have to be you?''

''Because she asked me.''

He studied her for a long moment. ''Is it because Erin asked you to help her, or because Jerrod asked you to help her?''

''What difference does it make to you?'' she snapped, fighting the old familiar defensiveness her eldest brother had always wrought in her. ''You've never been involved in my life before, so why not stay out of it now?''

He stood, a frown of irritation creasing his forehead. ''I don't know, I had some stupid idea that family members worry about one another, but you make it damned hard to offer you any support.''

Without waiting for her reply, he turned and

strode out of the office. Johnna stared at the empty doorway, her stomach knotted into a tense ball.

Jerrod was a minister. Erin had asked for her help, and her brother had offered her his support. Johnna felt as if somehow the world had tilted and sent everything topsy-turvy. And for the first time in a very long time, she felt vulnerable and afraid of the changes occurring in her life.

It was almost nine the next evening when Jerrod drove past Johnna's law office and saw her car parked out front and the lights on in the office.

Jerrod was at the end of a busy day. He'd spent the morning signing the final papers that would make the house across the street from Johnna's his own. The afternoon had sped by as he'd begun packing up a lifetime of his father's things in boxes and crates.

Although the deal on the house wouldn't officially close for another two weeks, the owners had agreed to let him and his father move in immediately, and it was a move Jerrod was eager to make. He had to get his father out of that trailer and away from the crippling memories contained within.

On impulse, Jerrod pulled his car into the space next to Johnna's and shut off his engine. He thought of Johnna's reaction when she'd seen him at the house across the street.

It had amused him how unsubtle she had been in attempting to get him to buy someplace else. Her reaction had also intrigued him, letting him know she wasn't as indifferent to him as she'd pretended.

It hadn't been the location of the house that had prompted him to buy it, but rather that the place had been on the market for quite some time. It obviously needed work and the owners were desperate to sell. The price had been right, and its being across the street from Johnna's place had simply been an unexpected boon.

He knew that as busy as his day had been, Johnna's had been just as busy. Erin's arraignment had been that morning, and Jerrod had heard through the prolific grapevine that Johnna had been successful in getting Erin out on bail.

As he climbed out of his car, he wondered if Johnna had been here all afternoon and evening. She probably hadn't even stopped for dinner. Even as a teenager, she'd never taken care of herself. She'd focus her energy on an injustice or a cause and forget to eat and sleep.

And in this particular instance, he felt partially responsible, in that he had been instrumental in getting her to agree to represent Erin.

He tried the front door, not surprised to find it locked, then knocked. He saw her come out of an inner office, her eyes widening slightly as she saw him.

"Jerrod—what are you doing here?" she said as she opened the door to allow him inside.

"I was driving by and saw the lights and figured

you probably worked through dinner. Have you eaten?''

She shook her head. "I'm not hungry."

"You have to eat, Johnna. It's going to be a long trial. Come on, let the new preacher in town treat you to dinner at the diner."

"Jerrod, I don't think—"

"That's right," he interjected quickly. "You can't think on an empty stomach. Come on, lock up and let's get a bite to eat."

She hesitated a moment, then acquiesced. "Let me grab my purse," she said.

A moment later they walked down the sidewalk toward the only lights that remained lit on Main Street. The diner would be open for another half hour or so, then it, too, would join the darkened businesses that surrounded it.

The heat of the day had ebbed only slightly, and despite the scent of hot sidewalk and asphalt, Jerrod could smell the sweet, floral scent of her that had haunted him for months after he'd left Inferno behind.

"I understand congratulations are in order," he said.

"Congratulations? You mean about getting Erin bail?" She frowned. "It's just the first battle in a long war. Save your congratulations for when I successfully defend her against all the charges."

"And what do you think the odds of that happening are?" he asked.

She shrugged. "Too early to tell. First thing in

the morning I'm going to the crime scene to look around. I've already got Judd Stevens gathering what information he can, but it will probably be weeks before I get any reports from him.''

''And when is the trial scheduled to begin?''

Her frown deepened. ''August fifteenth. I was hoping for at least a couple of months, but Judge Wellsby hates me and I think he set the trial date three weeks from now just to make things as difficult as possible for me.''

''Why does he hate you?'' he asked curiously.

For just a moment her eyes sparkled and her chin lifted with a familiar burst of defiance. ''He thinks I'm impertinent and stubborn and a pain.''

''And are you?''

A whisper of a smile curved the corners of her mouth. ''Of course I am. It's what makes me a good lawyer.''

They stopped talking as Jerrod opened the door to the diner. Inside there were only three patrons— an old man sipping coffee at the counter and a young couple in a booth nearby.

Jerrod led her to the third booth on the left side of the establishment, realizing only after they were seated that this was where they had always sat when they'd been teenagers.

At that time Jerrod had been perfectly satisfied to sit and stare at Johnna, to lose himself in the sooty gray of her eyes, the sweet curve of her lips and the memories of the lovemaking they'd just shared.

However, Jerrod knew they were not those same

two people. They had been foolish teenagers playing at love, unaware of how complicated emotions and passions could get in the grown-up world.

And on the night that drama unfolded, tragedy occurred and emotions flared out of control. The love that Johnna and Jerrod thought would sustain them through everything fell apart.

He shoved those memories aside, knowing there was no reason to go back to the night when his life had irrevocably shattered.

After months of self-destructive anger, of wallowing in self-pity and recriminations, his soul-searching and faith had finally brought him to a place of peace he wasn't willing to relinquish to the power of memories.

"You look tired, Johnna," he said.

She smiled wryly. "You're some sweet talker, Preacher man." She raked a hand through her short hair, the tousled style merely adding to her attractiveness. "I worked late at the ranch last night to make sure I got my hours in for this week."

"Who keeps track of your hours?" Jerrod asked curiously.

"The original executor of father's will was Walter Tilley, and he pretty much had us on an honor system. Unfortunately Walter had a little side business of running illegal aliens through the old barn at the ranch. He's now in prison awaiting trial on a variety of charges. The court appointed a new executor, and he's installed a time clock in the office."

"So you punch in and out when you're at the ranch?" Jerrod asked incredulously.

She nodded. "Crazy, huh? Kind of like working at a fast-food place, only without the benefits."

"And you have to do this for how long?"

"A year."

"And what happens when the year is up?"

She unfolded her napkin and placed it in her lap. "I'm not sure. I mean, the ranch will be ours, but I don't know what my brothers will want to do. I wouldn't mind selling the place and splitting the proceeds, but I can't imagine them wanting to do that."

"I hear your friend came into town," he said after they'd placed their orders.

She smiled, a quick burst of light on her features that made an answering warmth sweep through him. "Harriet. She arrived first thing yesterday morning."

"She's a good friend of yours?" he asked. Funny, he didn't remember Johnna having friends years ago. Adam Delaney didn't allow his children to have friends. For the first couple of months of Johnna and Jerrod's relationship, they had only been able to meet when she could sneak out of the house.

"Without Harriet Smith, I probably would never have made it through college and law school." She took a sip of her water, her eyes the darkest gray he'd ever seen. "I think sometimes she saved not only my sanity, but my life."

He leaned forward. "What do you mean?"

"It isn't important." She waved her hands to dismiss her words. "I was just dealing with a lot of issues, and Harriet helped me make sense of them."

"Was I one of those issues?" Jerrod asked softly.

"Don't flatter yourself," she replied with a distinct edge to her voice. She swallowed whatever else she was going to say as the waitress appeared with their order.

Suddenly Jerrod felt the need to go backward, to talk about their shared past, about his betrayal of her and the acrimony of their final parting. There was unfinished business between them, but he wasn't certain what that unfinished business was.

"Johnna, about what happened years ago..."

She held up a hand, her face a mask of stone. "Don't, Jerrod."

"But I think we should talk about it," he protested.

"Why? Talking about it won't change anything. I make it a practice to never look back. It's counterproductive. Besides—" she picked up a potato chip from her plate "—I have more than enough on my plate in the here and now."

"And I can't tell you how grateful I am that you took Erin's case."

She nodded and for a few minutes they focused on their food and didn't speak. It wasn't an uncomfortable silence; rather, it was reminiscent of the companionable silences they'd shared long ago.

Johnna had never been one of those women who needed to fill a silence with words. If she had nothing worthwhile to say, she remained quiet. Jerrod had always admired that about her, as he, too, had long ago learned the value of silent introspection.

They finished the meal and began the walk back to her office, where their cars were parked. They exchanged small talk as they walked, discussing some of the new businesses that had popped up on Main Street and what businesses were no longer there.

They had reached their cars when she stopped and looked up at him, curiosity lighting her eyes. "Why did you come back here, Jerrod? You always talked like if you ever left Inferno, you'd never return."

He smiled. "The words of an angry, bitter young man. When I was here, I hated everything about Inferno. I hated the heat, I hated the buildings, but most of all, I hated the people who I believed had let me down, allowed me to be the trailer-trash hoodlum they expected me to be."

He leaned against the front bumper of his car, remembering those months after he'd left Inferno. "It took a long time for me to realize that the hatred I harbored inside was hurting only one person—myself."

He stepped forward, wanting her to understand what forces had brought him back to this place of such misery and unhappiness. "I came back here because I needed to face the people I once hated with love and forgiveness. I came back because I know there are teenagers like Erin and I were—

throwaway kids—who just need a break. I intend for a large part of my ministry to be a youth group.''

''And then there's your father,'' she said.

Jerrod frowned. ''Yes, there is my father.'' Forgiving his father for his weaknesses had been nearly as difficult as Jerrod's forgiving himself. ''I've reached a peace where he's concerned, as well.''

''I'm glad for you.'' In the light shining from the nearby street lamp, Jerrod thought she'd never looked more lovely. She peered down at her wristwatch. ''I should go. It's getting late and I have a busy day scheduled for tomorrow.''

She turned to go to her car, but Jerrod stopped her by taking her arm. ''Johnna?''

He wasn't sure what he wanted or why he'd stopped her until she turned to look at him, her eyes puzzled and her mouth opened slightly.

Then he knew exactly what he wanted. As he stepped forward and captured her mouth with his, his last conscious thought was that he'd lied to her.

When he'd told her all the reasons he'd returned to Inferno, he'd committed a lie of omission. He hadn't told her, hadn't realized until this moment that he'd returned to Inferno for this—for her.

Chapter 5

He might be a minister, but he kissed like a man. His mouth plied hers with sinful heat, and for just a moment Johnna allowed herself to fall into the familiar, combustible fire.

As his tongue pushed into her mouth, deepening the intimacy of the kiss, she heard the pounding of a heart and wasn't sure if it was his or hers.

She only knew that time hadn't diminished the absolute power of Jerrod's kiss. Time hadn't lessened his mastery of sensual pleasure. Suddenly Johnna's mind was filled with memories of Jerrod's hands caressing her body, the feel of his naked skin against hers and the heights of pleasure to which he'd taken her.

She gasped and stepped away from him, frightened by the evocative pull of those memories. ''You shouldn't have done that,'' she said, appalled to hear her voice so breathless and trembling.

"Perhaps I shouldn't have,'' he agreed softly. "But I couldn't help myself.''

"Then pray for strength,'' she said, "because it won't happen again.'' She sighed and raked a hand through her hair. "I told you before, Jerrod. I can't revisit the past, and you are my past. Especially now, I can't go back. Not if I want to provide Erin with the best possible counsel.''

She got into her car, grateful when he didn't stop her and didn't attempt to say more.

Her hands still trembled as she pulled away from the office and drove off toward her house. Her mouth felt the vivid imprint of his, and her heart banged a harsh, unsteady rhythm.

How did he still have the power to affect her so with just a kiss? How could the mere act of pressing his lips against hers cause her heart to race uncontrollably, her knees to weaken and desire to throb inside her?

She could not allow Jerrod back in her life. No matter how mesmerizing she found the blue of his eyes, no matter how compelling she found his inner peace and strength, no matter how provocative she found his touch, his kiss.

There was no room for a man in the life she had chosen for herself, she thought as she parked her car and went into her house. Especially the man who had once owned every part of her and had callously thrown it all away.

She locked the front door, then walked through the dark living room and into her bedroom. Turning on the lamp, she sank onto the bed, her mind still reeling from the trauma of kissing Jerrod.

She'd had enough men in her life to last a lifetime. Her father, the man who should have made her feel safe and secure, loved and wanted, had never let her forget his disappointment in her very existence.

Her childhood had consisted of mental and verbal abuse. Although her father had never beaten her the way he'd beaten his sons, he'd battered her with cruel, abusive words. He'd told her she was stupid and worthless and would never amount to anything.

By the time she'd become a teenager, she was angry and had a well of hurt inside her that crippled her soul. The ranch she'd loved had become a place she hated, filled with tension and abuse.

Then she'd hooked up with Jerrod, a young man who had a reputation for trouble. He, too, had a well of anger and hurt inside him created by a childhood with an absent mother, an alcoholic father and a town who shunned him.

Together they'd spun magic. Their love reached inside and healed wounds, gave confidence and built dreams. Jerrod's love had washed away the pain her father had inflicted, and she had blossomed beneath his love, certain that theirs was a shining future of happily-ever-after.

Then Jerrod had shattered the magic by sleeping with Erin McCall and in the process destroyed any illusion Johnna had had of love and happily-ever-after.

She would never again trust any man. She would never again allow a man into her heart. She had learned her lesson well.

She leaned down and opened the bottom drawer of her nightstand. Inside the drawer was an old cardboard box. She pulled out the box, set it on the bed next to her, then opened it.

Her heart cried out as she saw the tiny pink gown that lay inside. She pulled it out and raised it to her face. Drawing a deep breath, she thought she could still smell the faint scent of baby lotion and powder.

"Miranda," she whispered, tears burning her eyes. Her arms ached with the memory of holding her tiny daughter. Her heart ached with the memory of bright blue eyes that had gazed at her with absolute trust.

It had been a difficult birth—twenty hours of intense labor and the knowledge that it was far too early for the baby to come. Miranda lived for three days.

Johnna buried her baby girl alone, overwhelmed with grief and a guilt that tore at her insides. And on that day, standing alone at the tiny grave, she vowed she would never again allow a man in her life.

"I'm sorry," she whispered, then placed the gown back into the box and returned the box to the drawer, her heart hardened by these memories.

If any weakness for Jerrod ever entered her mind,

all she needed to do was take out this box and remind herself of the tragedy she'd suffered alone.

Strengthened by her pain, she undressed, got into bed and slept without dreams until her alarm went off the next morning.

At nine o'clock Johnna and Harriet met Erin in Erin's room at the bed-and-breakfast, where Harriet was also staying. "We have very little time to come up with a reasonable defense," Johnna said to the slender, pale-haired woman. "And the best way to cast reasonable doubt on your guilt is to have a reasonable alternative theory to offer the jury."

"An alternative theory?" Erin frowned.

"What we need to know, dear, is who else might have wanted your husband dead," Harriet explained.

Erin's frown deepened. "I...I wouldn't even know how to begin to answer that. I know Richard had business adversaries, but I can't imagine any of his business dealings becoming so personal that somebody would want to kill him."

"But somebody did kill him. Somebody bashed in his head," Johnna said. "Those blows took a lot of hate, a lot of rage, and you need to figure out who might have hated Richard enough to accomplish such an up-close-and-personal murder."

Erin raised her chin, her gaze meeting Johnna's. "And we know it wasn't me," she said as if needing to confirm her innocence once again.

Johnna nodded. "And we know it wasn't you,"

she agreed. Johnna had absolutely no reason in the world to believe Erin, yet she did.

Despite any residual bitterness she might feel for the woman who had been party to Jerrod's betrayal, Johnna believed in her gut that Erin had not killed her husband.

Johnna handed her a legal pad and a pen. "What I need you to do is make a list of everyone you knew Richard was having any sort of problems with—co-workers, employees, business associates or neighbors."

"How far back should I go?"

Johnna frowned thoughtfully. "As far as you can remember. You never know how the past might affect the present."

Erin nodded solemnly and got to work.

Later, after Johnna had consulted with Harriet alone and left the two women in their respective rooms, her words to Erin haunted her.

Could the past affect the present? Perhaps in Erin's case, but Johnna certainly didn't intend to allow her past to have anything at all to do with her present.

She'd just exited the bed-and-breakfast when she ran smack-dab into Jerrod, who was on his way inside. He caught her by the shoulders. "Whoa!" he exclaimed as he steadied her.

"Sorry," she said. "I didn't see you. My mind was a million miles away." She was grateful when he dropped his hands to his sides. "Are you here to see Erin?"

A dark eyebrow rose in surprise. "Actually I was looking for you. I didn't know Erin was here."

"The police still have her house under wrap, and in any case, she didn't want to go back there. We got her a room here for the duration of the trial." She shifted her briefcase from beneath one arm to the other. "Why were you looking for me?"

"To offer my help."

"Your help? What are you going to do? Pray for me to win the case?" Her tone was dry.

He grinned. "I've already begun that. What I had in mind was a more active kind of help."

"What do you mean?" she asked. Funny how the thought that she was in Jerrod's prayers touched her heart.

"I know you have a small office and only a secretary for help. I also know you don't have much time to gather facts, so I'm offering myself to the defense team. I didn't think you took my previous offer to help seriously, but I am serious."

Johnna's initial reaction was to tell him that she didn't need his help, that she could handle things fine on her own. But she owed Erin the best possible defense, and the more people she had helping, the better the odds of success.

Besides, she refused to consider that she was afraid of being around him, that his closeness in any capacity might make her weak, might make her want him again.

"If you're serious about the offer, I was just on my way to the crime scene. Want to tag along?"

"Sure," he instantly agreed.

A few minutes later as Johnna drove to the Kramer mansion, she almost regretted her invitation to Jerrod. Jerrod filled the small confines of the car with his bewitching male scent and his magnetic presence.

"You haven't been to the crime scene?" he asked.

"No, I haven't had time since taking the case. According to the sheriff, they're all finished with their investigation at the scene and have only kept it closed off for any defense team that might want to come in. One of the deputies will meet us there to let us in."

"What are we looking for?"

"I don't know," Johnna admitted. "Something the police might have missed, something that might shift the finger of accusation away from Erin."

"Johnna." She felt the weight of his gaze on her, but she kept her gaze firmly fixed on the road ahead. "I know this can't be easy on you, that it would have been easier if the person you were defending was anyone but Erin."

"I told you before, Jerrod. I don't have a problem with Erin." What she didn't say was that her problem had always been with him. He was the one who had betrayed her. He was the one who had broken their trust, their vows of love forevermore. And for that, she would never, ever forgive him.

Erin Kramer had obviously married well. As Johnna pulled up before the two-story mansion with

the sweeping porch, elaborate columns and mani-
cured yard, Jerrod thought of how far his friend had
come from the trailer park.

Unfortunately, from what he'd learned of her marriage, she'd sacrificed her soul for a fancy home
with all the trappings. His heart hurt for his old
friend and the circumstances she now found herself
in.

"Nice place," he observed as they got out of
Johnna's car.

"One of the nicest in town."

"A bit isolated, isn't it?"

Johnna looked around, then nodded. "Isolated
enough so that no neighbors would have heard anything the night of the murder." She looked at her
wristwatch. "We've got a few minutes before one
of the deputies arrives to let us in. Want to sit on
the porch?"

"Sure, at least it's in the shade." Although it was
just after ten in the morning, the heat already shim-
mered in the air and pressed in on him.

A moment later they were sitting on the two white
wicker chairs on the porch. Jerrod glanced at
Johnna, who was looking over some notes on a legal
pad.

This morning she was clad in a pair of tailored
beige knee-length shorts, a navy blouse and a beige
suit jacket. The blue of the blouse made her eyes
appear more blue than gray.

It was early enough in the day that she should

still look fresh and rested from a good night's sleep. But instead, her hair looked as if it had been only finger-combed, and her lips were compressed together in a taut line. Beneath her eyes was a slight red puffiness that attested to a restless night.

Tenderness stole through him. He wanted to pull her into his arms, hold her against him and ease some of the stress that simmered inside her. He remembered how fully she'd always thrown herself into any project. He also remembered how at one time her project had been him.

She'd come to him with an intensity that had been breathtaking and awe-inspiring. She'd consumed him and he'd allowed it, meeting her with the same sort of consumptive hunger.

And he'd destroyed them.

But last night when he'd kissed her, he'd felt an old familiar flame in the pit of his stomach—the fire of want, the heat of desire. It had been almost nine years since he'd felt it and he welcomed it. He realized there had always been only one woman for him, and that woman was sitting next to him.

But once again the specter of Erin was between them. Johnna had made it clear that she didn't intend to delve into their past and his betrayal. And yet he knew there was no real hope for the two of them until they could resolve the past.

Until last night she'd insisted there was nothing to resolve, that all was forgotten. But after he'd kissed her, when she'd told him she couldn't go back to the past and still provide Erin with a good defense, he'd realized there was still a load of baggage concerning the events of all those years ago.

He was confident God had forgiven him, and he'd long ago forgiven himself, but he wondered what it would take for Johnna to forgive him.

His attention was drawn to the road, where a plume of dust forecasted the approach of a car. Both he and Johnna stood as a patrol car pulled into the driveway.

A young deputy stepped out. "Good morning, Johnna," he said, then nodded to Jerrod.

"Hi, Charlie," Johnna replied. "This is Jerrod McCain, he's the new minister in town. Jerrod, this is Charlie Witworth, Inferno's youngest deputy."

Charlie blushed and pulled a key chain from his pocket. "I might be young, but I take my job seriously." He unlocked the front door of the Kramer house and stepped aside for Jerrod and Johnna to enter.

"Thanks, Charlie. We'll take it from here. We'll lock up when we're finished," Johnna said.

Charlie's face grew more crimson. "Uh...I'm supposed to stay here until you're done."

Johnna frowned. "You've got to be kidding. Is Sheriff Broder afraid we'll steal something?"

"Come on, Johnna, don't give me a hard time. I'm just following orders." It was obvious from the pained expression on the young man's face that he had either experienced firsthand or knew secondhand about Johnna's legendary temper.

"Why don't we get started?" Jerrod suggested.

Johnna hesitated a moment, then nodded curtly, and together the three of them walked from the marble-floored entryway into an elegant, spacious living room.

The room would have been beautiful if not for the chalk outline, the large bloodstain on the floor and the overturned furniture that gave evidence of a brawl.

Jerrod said nothing as he watched Johnna walk slowly around the room. She touched nothing, spoke not a word, but he could tell she was taking in and mentally processing all that the room had to offer.

"You responded the night of the murder?" she asked Charlie.

He nodded. "Yeah, I was here."

"And everything looked just as it does now? The end table was overturned, the broken glass on the floor?"

Jerrod followed her gaze to the broken crystal next to the toppled end table. He instantly recognized the figurine that lay shattered on the floor. It had been a crystal angel he'd stolen from a local card shop and given to Erin for her fourteenth birthday.

It touched him deeply that Erin had kept the gift all this time. He vowed again to do whatever he could to help her. There was no way he would ever believe she could cold-bloodedly bludgeon a man to death.

"Everything looks the same," Charlie replied.

"Except of course all the fingerprint dust. We left that behind."

"Prints were lifted?" Jerrod asked.

"Richard's and Erin's prints were on several surfaces, but the cleaning lady had been in that day and we couldn't find anyone else's prints anywhere," Charlie explained.

Johnna frowned and walked from the living room into the bright, airy kitchen. Jerrod followed and Charlie brought up the rear.

She barely glanced at anything in the kitchen, but instead, headed directly into the laundry room. There on the top of the dryer was a navy-blue shirt marred with a sprinkling of white lint.

"Just like Erin said," Johnna commented more to herself than to anyone else. "The inciting incident—a shirt with lint." She left the laundry room and went back into the living room, her gaze darting here and there, assessing everything.

For the next hour and a half, Jerrod and Johnna searched the living room and kitchen. They looked in cabinets, under cushions and in drawers. Neither was sure what they were looking for, but Jerrod knew Johnna wouldn't be satisfied until she was certain the rooms held no clues, no evidence of another killer.

She turned to Charlie, her eyes dark and fathomless. "I want to see the rest of the house."

Charlie shrugged. "I don't see why. All the action took place right here in the living room."

"You might as well indulge her, Charlie," Jerrod

said. "If she gets it into her head she's going to see the rest of the house, then it will take nothing short of a miracle to stop her."

"And miracles are in short supply in Inferno," Johnna added, then headed for the stairs with the men trailing behind her.

The upstairs was as beautifully decorated as the lower level. Each bedroom had a specific color scheme. There was one in shades of blue, one in lush lavender, and the master suite was decorated in shades of sunny yellow. Each room appeared to be in meticulous order, with nothing out of place or suspicious-looking.

It took only minutes to go through the spare rooms and discern that there was nothing personal stored in any of the dressers or closets.

Johnna lingered in the master suite, looking into drawers and closets. Jerrod worked with her, admiring her ability to focus so intently and unable to help but appreciate the shapely length of her legs.

"The only thing we collected from this room was Richard Kramer's address book," Charlie said. "Can you tell me what you're looking for?" he asked in obvious agitation as she began to check the shoe boxes that lined the late Richard Kramer's closet shelf.

"No," Johnna said curtly, opening the second box of many. "I can't tell you because I don't know. My goodness, I thought only women had this kind of shoe obsession."

Charlie shifted from one foot to the other. "It

doesn't seem quite right, digging around everywhere.''

''Yeah, well, it doesn't seem quite right that an innocent woman is being charged for murdering Richard.''

Charlie said nothing as they got back to work. As Jerrod peeked into each of the nightstands, he realized that each drawer contained a piece of the personalities of Erin and Richard Kramer.

Richard's nightstand held a jar of hard candy, a hunting magazine and a handgun, leaving the impression of a redneck macho guy with a sweet tooth.

Erin's nightstand drawers held a variety of perfumed lotions, a romance novel and several sets of earplugs. Apparently the late Richard Kramer snored.

Jerrod finished with the nightstands, then sat on the edge of the bed and watched as Johnna continued to look in the shoe boxes.

He wondered what he might be able to discern about *her* if he snooped in all her drawers and cabinets. What did she keep near her in her nightstand drawers? Somehow he didn't think he'd find romance novels.

The woman she'd become in the years since they'd been apart seemed too hardened to believe in the magic of love. She probably kept legal books and briefs in her nightstand.

''Bingo!'' Johnna exclaimed, and stood with a shoe box in her hand. She left the closet and crossed to Jerrod. The box held old photographs, yellowed newspaper clippings and what appeared to be love letters. "I knew there had to be personal items somewhere."

"Looks like a bunch of old junk to me," Charlie said.

"Then you won't mind if I take it with me?" Johnna asked.

Charlie shrugged. "It don't matter to me. I'll let the sheriff know you took it."

She nodded, placed the lid on the shoe box, then stood. "I guess we're finished here." She sounded a bit frustrated.

Jerrod touched her arm lightly. "Maybe that P.I. Judd Stevens will turn up something you can use." He knew she'd hoped to find something—anything—that she could use in Erin's defense. But the crime scene had yielded virtually nothing.

"I hope you're right," she replied. She tucked the box beneath her arm. "Let's get out of here."

They said goodbye to Charlie, then got back into Johnna's car. She started the engine, but instead of putting the car into gear and taking off, she opened the shoe box and began to pull out the items one by one.

The first thing she pulled out was a wedding picture of Erin and Richard. "They certainly started out looking happy enough," she said as she handed the photo to him.

Jerrod looked at the photo of the smiling couple, and for just a moment it wasn't a picture of Erin and Richard, but of him standing next to Johnna in a silk-and-lace white dress.

They had spoken often about getting married. They'd planned the ceremony, plotted their shared future and built dreams. Two children, they'd decided so long ago, and a house with a fenced-in yard and a big furry dog.

Suddenly his head was filled with thoughts of the kiss they had shared the night before, a kiss that had kept him sleepless most of the night. Her lips had been every bit as sweet, as hot and as inviting, as he'd remembered.

"What's this?"

His attention returned to what Johnna was doing. "What?"

"This news article." She frowned. "I don't remember this." She held it out to him and instantly a chill danced up his spine as he read the headline: Woman Slain in Trailer Park.

He watched as she scanned the article. "Why would Erin and Richard have a news clipping concerning Tabitha Warren's murder?" she asked incredulously. "The other clippings here are about the same story."

"Tabitha Warren was Erin's mother."

Johnna stared at him as if he'd suddenly spoken in a foreign language. "Erin's mother was murdered nine years ago?"

He nodded, and wondered if Johnna would be able to figure out that the night Tabitha Warren was beaten to death was the same night he'd betrayed Johnna by sleeping with Erin.

Death and betrayal. Even after all these years, it still left a bad taste in his mouth.

Chapter 6

"I don't understand why Richard Kramer would keep newspaper clippings of Erin's mother's death," Johnna said as she speared another French fry with her fork.

She and Jerrod were seated across from each other at the table in her kitchen. After leaving the Kramer house, Johnna had driven back to the bed-and-breakfast and asked Erin about the shoe box.

Erin had been totally shocked by the news clippings about her mother's death and had no idea why Richard would have them hidden away in his closet.

"I mean, don't you find it rather, I don't know, ghoulish?" she asked Jerrod now.

"Definitely odd," Jerrod agreed as he added mustard to his hamburger. "Maybe he was just curious about it."

"If you're curious, you go to the library and pull up the reports. You don't keep clippings in a shoe box in your closet," Johnna replied.

She wasn't sure why she'd invited him into her house and offered to cook dinner. He'd picked up his car at the bed-and-breakfast and she could have just let them part ways there. She wanted to believe that her invitation was because she was enjoying the mental volleying between them as they discussed different aspects of the case.

For a minister, Jerrod made a good devil's advocate. For each scenario she came up with concerning what had happened that night in the Kramer house, he countered with an argument that destroyed the abstract she'd come up with.

The only thing he couldn't explain away was the nine-year-old news clippings concerning the murder of Tabitha Warren.

She was feeling a sense of security where he was concerned. They had spent much of the day together, and there had been no conversational slips into their personal past, no indication that he was anything more than a concerned minister helping in the defense of an old friend.

"I'm calling Sheriff Broder in the morning. I want to get all the files and reports concerning Erin's mother's murder," Johnna said thoughtfully.

Jerrod smiled the old familiar smile that caused a starburst of heat in the pit of her stomach. "One murder case isn't enough? You need to open another one?"

She frowned. "It bothers me that Richard had those clippings. It doesn't fit. And things that don't fit bother me."

"Surely you don't think there's any connection between Richard's murder and Tabitha's murder." He finished the last bite of his hamburger and shoved his plate aside. "What could be the possible connection?"

"I don't know. I don't know what to think." She picked up the last French fry on her plate and popped it into her mouth. She chewed thoughtfully, thinking of the newspaper articles detailing Tabitha Warren's murder.

"Did you know Erin's mother?" she asked.

He nodded.

"Tell me about her."

Jerrod frowned with concentration. "She was pretty and young and sad. She spent much of her time down at the Honky Tonk, drinking too much and bringing home men. I think she was desperate and hated to be alone."

"How did she get along with Erin?"

"They fought a lot. Erin was embarrassed by her mother's promiscuity, ashamed of her drinking and carrying on. Erin and her mother had a huge fight the night Tabitha was killed."

Johnna gazed at him curiously. "You remember that night?"

Again he nodded, his expression unreadable. "It was just after supper the night that Erin came over upset because of a fight with her mother. There's a huge old rock behind the trailer park. Erin and I went there. We'd often go there to talk. From the rock you couldn't see the trailer park, couldn't see much of anything except the sky overhead and the empty desert.''

He leaned back in the chair, his gaze not quite meeting hers. ''We were there for hours. She talked about how much she hated her life with her mother, and I talked about how much I hated my life with my father. We plotted and planned how each of us would eventually leave the trailer park and Inferno far behind, how someday everyone who had called us trailer trash and looked down on us would be sorry.''

He smiled and shook his head ruefully. ''We were so young and so filled with the unfairness of our lives. We were there until just after dark. Then I told her I had to go, that I knew you'd be able to get away from the ranch soon and I was to meet you.''

A wave of memories assailed Johnna. How eager she used to be each night for her father to make his way to bed. It was only after Adam Delaney went to sleep that she would sneak out her window and meet Jerrod at the end of the lane that led to the ranch.

''Anyway,'' Jerrod continued, ''Erin and I parted ways just in front of our trailers. I stood on my porch and watched her disappear into hers, then heard a bloodcurdling scream. I raced over there and found Tabitha on the living-room floor, obviously dead.''

"You called the sheriff?" Johnna asked.

"I did. Later the medical examiner determined that she had probably been killed an hour or so before Erin found her."

"Was the killer caught?"

"No—at least not that I know of. Although, you have to remember, within a week of the murder, I left Inferno. It's quite possible the murder was solved and I never heard about it."

Johnna stood and grabbed their plates, carrying them to the sink. Jerrod did likewise with the silverware and glasses.

"Don't you think it's weird that Erin's mother was beaten about the head with an object that was never found? Just like Richard was." She spoke as she rinsed the dishes, then handed them to him for loading into the dishwasher.

She steadfastly refused to dwell on the intimacy of the domestic scene, how often in her youth she'd imagined them doing such simple things as washing dishes side by side.

"Coffee?" she asked.

"Sure," he said. "Weird yes, coincidence probably," he continued. "Unless you think there might be a serial killer here in Inferno who only gets the urge to kill every nine years or so."

"Very funny," she said. She didn't speak again until the coffee was dripping into the carafe of the coffeemaker. She leaned against the cabinet and looked at Jerrod. "I think you and I are the only people in town who believe in Erin's innocence.

Even my brother, Matthew, thinks she did it. But of course if I said the sky is blue, Matthew would insist it was green.''

Je   laughed. "You have never realized how lucky you are to have siblings. I always wanted a brother or a sister.''

"Trust me, the sibling thing is vastly overrated.'' She poured them each a cup of coffee, then gestured toward the living room. "Let's sit in there where we'll be more comfortable.''

He nodded and followed her from the kitchen. They sat on the sofa and she placed the steaming mugs of coffee on coasters on the table in front of them.

Jerrod picked up his cup and leaned back against the overstuffed burgundy cushions, looking far too attractive. "I like your place, Johnna. It's the kind of place where I always imagined you'd live.''

"What do you mean?'' she asked curiously.

"It's cozy, yet stylish. You always loved burgundy and you always said when you got your own place you'd have a burgundy sofa and lots of real green plants.'' He gestured to the plant stand by the window.

"Those are my pets, my family and my relationships,'' she said, looking at the lush greenery. "They give me pleasure yet demand very little from me.''

"But they must be uncomfortable to sleep with,'' he replied. "I mean, they can't exactly hold you when you need comfort or warm you on a cold night.''

"I comfort myself when I need it, and Inferno never gets cold at night," she retorted. "And I think it's highly inappropriate for the new minister in town to be talking about my sleeping companions."

"Ah, but it's my job to minister not only to spiritual needs, but also the emotional needs of my flock." His eyes gleamed provocatively.

"I don't consider myself one of your flock," she returned, aware that somehow the conversation had veered into an area far too personal for her liking. "And I have no emotional needs." She picked up her cup of coffee and sipped, her gaze still lingering on him. "Why a minister, Jerrod?" It was a question that had nagged at her since the moment she'd seen him at the church for Mark's wedding. "Of all the things I imagined you choosing to become, a minister certainly wasn't one of them."

"It wasn't so much I chose it as it chose me." His gaze went to the far wall, and she could see that he was drifting back in time. "When I got to Dallas, I stayed with a friend of Uncle Cyrus'—a preacher named John Caldicott." He drew a deep breath. "And I was angry at the world." He gazed at her for a long moment, his eyes dark and thoughtful. She wondered if he was remembering the words she'd said to him the final time she'd seen him.

They had been words intended to wound, words intended to hurt him as deeply as he had hurt her. She hadn't pulled any punches, but had hit him below the belt, knowing where he was most vulnerable.

"I spent the first year of my time in Dallas drinking too much, searching for trouble and finding it more often than not. The good Reverend Caldicott said nothing. Every night I came home drunk, disorderly, obnoxious and spoiling for a fight, and he never said a word."

"So what turned things around?" she asked. Despite the fact that she tried to tell herself she didn't care, she was intrigued to learn what had happened to him after he'd left Inferno.

He paused a moment to take another sip of his coffee, set the cup back on the coffee table, then leaned forward.

She could smell him, that familiar male fragrance that set her pulse racing. His deep blue eyes beckoned her to follow wherever he led.

"One night I was in a bar—some dive I'd never been in before. As usual I had drunk too much and was mouthing off like I had no brains. It was almost closing time when I left, and I found a gang of men waiting for me. They grabbed me, pulled me into an alley and proceeded to give me the beating of my life."

He closed his eyes and winced as if remembering the pain of the beating, and Johnna had to fight the impulse to reach out to him. As much as she wished to offer him a bit of comfort, she knew that to touch him in any way was dangerous.

The moment he'd kissed her the night before,

she'd recognized how vulnerable she still was to their physical attraction. It would be far too easy for her to be overwhelmed by him, and she didn't intend to give him the chance, didn't want in any way to invite intimate personal contact.

When he opened his eyes once again, any memory of physical pain, any remnant of emotional trauma was gone, and his eyes were the clear, serene blue of summer skies. "As I lay in that alley, I thought I might be dying. And I recognized what a waste my life was.

"After a while I realized I wasn't going to die, and while I was waiting to get enough strength back to go home, I realized that the path I was on would lead eventually either to death or to prison.

"When I finally got home, Reverend Caldicott cleaned my wounds, applied ice packs and bandages, and he talked. And for the first time in my life, I listened. The next week I enrolled in college and vowed to turn my life around."

"And it was in college that you decided to become a minister?" she asked.

He nodded. "After taking several philosophy and theology classes, I knew the ministry was where I belonged."

There was a sense of strength emanating from him and a quiet peace that Johnna realized she envied. She had yet to feel as if she really belonged anywhere on this earth.

She started as he took her hands in his. "Come

to church on Sunday, Johnna,'' he said. ''Come and listen to my sermon.''

She pulled her hands from his and shook her head. ''I don't go to church,'' she replied.

''It's never too late to start.''

She stood, needing to distance herself from him, finding the light in his eyes, the scent of his cologne and the heat of his body far too provocative.

''It's getting late,'' she said pointedly. She suddenly wanted him out of her house. He looked far too comfortable on her sofa, as if he belonged there. And she didn't want even the merest whisper of his presence anywhere in this personal space of hers.

He stood and followed her to the front door, where he stood mere inches from her. He reached out and touched a short strand of her hair. ''When did you cut it all off?''

''When I got— A long time ago.'' She felt a flush heat her cheeks as she realized that she'd almost said *When I got pregnant.*

His hand lingered on the side of her face, warm and gentle. She fought a sudden need to lean into it, allow herself the simple pleasure of his touch.

''Your hair was pretty long, but it's pretty short, also.'' The blue of his eyes darkened to midnight and Johnna suddenly found it hard to breathe as she remembered those nights so long ago, when the deepening of his eye color was a prelude to foreplay.

''You were a beautiful teenager, and you've grown into a stunning woman,'' he said.

Although it had been less than twenty-four hours

since she told him kissing her was a mistake and she didn't want it to happen again, she now wanted him to kiss her. And she knew he was going to— by the heat in his gaze, by the slight, almost imperceptible quickening of his breathing as he took a step closer to her.

She knew she was inviting danger when she didn't step away from him, didn't do anything but part her lips slightly to welcome his kiss.

As his mouth moved over hers, her head filled with memories. They were sweet memories of laughter and innocence, of shared dreams and passionate embraces. Nine years of loneliness, of self-imposed isolation and a lack of emotional and physical contact heightened the memories.

She fell into his kiss, recognizing somewhere in the back of her mind that she suffered a lethal weakness where he was concerned. Despite the fact that she couldn't forgive him, she'd also never been able to forget him...or stop wanting him.

As his tongue dipped into her mouth, tangling with hers, she wrapped her arms around his neck, her fingers lightly stroking the hair at the nape of his neck.

At the same time, his arms pulled her tightly against the length of him and her body felt a homecoming as it molded to the familiar planes of his form.

She knew it was madness, but what she didn't understand was what sort of madness made her want him every bit as much as she thought she hated him.

* * *

Jerrod hadn't meant to kiss her, but he'd fought the desire to do so all day long. The brief kiss they'd shared the night before had only managed to whet his appetite.

As he pulled her closely into him, able to feel the press of her full breasts against his chest, wild desire swooped through him.

Her mouth tasted both of sweet memories and thrilling freshness, and Jerrod found himself being swept to a height of pleasure he hadn't experienced for nine long years.

She was fire—sizzling in his veins, burning all his nerve endings with flaming sensation. Still keeping her mouth captive with his, he maneuvered them away from the door and toward the sofa.

She didn't protest the move, didn't try to pull away as he eased them both down on the soft cushions. He left her lips and moved his mouth down the curve of her jaw, nibbling on the sensitive skin just below her ear.

He slid his hands up her slender back, then down once again. "Jerrod," she said softly. He didn't know if it was a protest or a plea, and instantly he stopped the movement of his hands. "Oh, Jerrod," she said, and this time he recognized the words as a plea.

His mouth sought hers again, and he felt himself falling deeper into her, his need for her growing, throbbing. When he moved his hands again, it was to gently cup her breasts. Their heat and the pebble hardness of her nipples pressed teasingly against the cotton material of her blouse.

She didn't discourage his touch, but rather leaned into him, arching her back as tiny gasps of pleasure escaped her lips.

It was all the encouragement Jerrod needed. His fingers nimbly worked on the buttons of her blouse. He wanted—needed—to touch her bare skin.

It took him only a few seconds to get the blouse unfastened and slide it off her shoulders, exposing the delicate lacy bra she wore beneath. He leaned back from her, his gaze taking in the bewitching sight of her soft gray eyes, her silky shoulders and the uppermost portion of her creamy breasts, which spilled over the top of the lace.

"Johnna, sweet Johnna. You are so beautiful," he whispered. He watched her eyes grow deeper in hue, the pleasure of his words obvious in the expression on her face.

He reached his arms around her once again and unfastened her bra. As he did so, her lips played along his throat. At the same time, her fingers danced over the buttons of his shirt, unfastening them hurriedly.

His senses spun like a top, making him dizzy, making rational thought impossible as her bra fell away and she shoved his shirt from his shoulders.

As she leaned into him and the hardened tips of her breasts grazed his chest, a vortex of desire threatened to pull him under and drown him. Her hands roamed the expanse of his back as if her fingertips were memorizing every detail.

He lay back, pulling her atop him, wanting to feel the length of her against him. Her heartbeat banged against his, each racing so fast it was impossible to discern one from the other.

Their mouths met once again, a joining tinged with a wildness without control. Unable to help himself, he moved his hips, grinding against hers in an unmistakable rhythm. She responded eagerly, moving her hips to meet each thrust of his.

Jerrod had never wanted anyone as much as he wanted her, but in some small part of his brain, he knew the timing was all wrong, and if they made love at this very moment, it would only complicate things between them.

Reluctantly, drawing on all the strength of character he possessed, he stopped any movement and withdrew his mouth from hers. Slowly he moved her off him and sat up. She gazed at him curiously, her eyes dazed from the sensual pleasure they had just shared.

"We can't do this, Johnna," he said. "This isn't the time for us yet."

She crossed her arms over her breasts, as if he'd just pointed out that she was sitting there half-naked. "I didn't want to do it—you just caught me off guard," she said as she reached for her bra and blouse and pulled them on.

"I apologize. I didn't mean for things to go so far," he said.

"I didn't intend for this even to begin," she replied, not looking at him. "You caught me at a weak moment. I'm tired and stressed."

He shook his head. "Don't."

"Don't what?"

"Don't make excuses for the fact that there's still something powerful between us." He leaned toward her. "You want to make love to me as much as I want to make love to you. There's still magic between us, Johnna. Even after all these years, there's still magic."

Her cheeks exploded with angry red as she stood. "Don't flatter yourself, Jerrod. There's no magic now and there wasn't any magic years ago. We were just two stupid kids hungry for affection who happened to connect. There is no magic anywhere. It was just a matter of hormones."

He stood and took her by the shoulders, forcing her to look into his face. "You're wrong, Johnna, and I intend to prove it to you. There *is* magic between us, but right now it's buried beneath the pain of our past. Eventually we're going to have to talk about what happened years ago, the things we said and did..."

She wrenched free of his grasp, walked to the front door and pulled it open. "My father taught me at a very early age that there was no Santa Claus, no tooth fairy, no magic in the entire world. For just a brief moment in time, you almost had me believing, but then you destroyed it. I told you before, I don't intend to talk or even think about the past. It's over and done.''

Pain radiated from every pore of her body, and for the first time Jerrod recognized the depth of the devastation he'd left behind when he'd escaped from Inferno. He'd done much more than only break her heart.

He leaned down, grabbed his shirt and pulled it on. As he buttoned it, he walked toward the door that she held open.

''Jerrod, I appreciate the help you're giving me on Erin's defense case, but you have to promise me that something like what just almost happened won't happen again. You have to promise me that you'll leave our past alone.''

He stood so close to her he could feel the heat that still radiated from her body. Her eyes were turbulent skies, a combination of pain, fear and lingering desire. She had never looked so vulnerable or so lovely.

Reaching up, he gently touched the side of her face, watched as her eyes grew impossibly dark. ''Sorry, Johnna, I can't make that promise.''

He dropped his hand and stepped outside. He walked to his car, aware that she remained at the door staring out at him.

As he backed out of the driveway, he wondered what on earth he was doing. Had he been led back to Inferno—back to Johnna—by a divine force with a mission to help heal the wounds he'd left behind?

He thought of the heat of her kisses, the sweet

feel of her silky skin against his own and how easily he'd nearly lost all control.

Was he on the path divined for him, or was it something quite different? Was he simply falling into temptation?

Chapter 7

Johnna wondered if lightning would strike her if she walked through the doors of the Inferno Methodist Church. She sat in her car and watched in amazement as every citizen of Inferno, it seemed, filed into the church.

The church hadn't been this well attended since the rumor had gone around that Iva Mae Caldwell intended to stand up and confess all her sins—and everyone in town knew Iva Mae sinned a lot.

Johnna got out of her car and joined the throng entering the house of worship. Apparently she wasn't the only one driven to come here to see the bad boy transformed into man of God.

She took a seat in a pew near the back of the church and picked up a hymnal. The organist was playing softly and people continued to arrive and take their seats. A sense of peace flooded through Johnna, as if the music and the tranquillity of the sanctuary found the rough spots inside her and smoothed them.

For the past week Johnna had been in turmoil. Not only had she been busy trying to formulate a defense for Erin and working the long hours out at the family ranch, she'd also spent the past week avoiding Jerrod.

And in the past week that had gotten more difficult. Three days earlier Jerrod and his father had begun moving into the house across the street. She'd watched them from her living-room window and tried to forget the kiss she and Jerrod had shared.

Even now, a full week later, she fought the memory of the taste of his mouth, the feel of his muscled chest, the heady sensations that had ripped through her with every touch of his fingers.

It was obvious to her that there was still a strong physical attraction between them. Intellectually, she could accept that she still felt an overwhelming desire for him. What she found herself wondering was if it was possible for her to indulge in a physical relationship with him and not give him any other part of her, no pieces of her heart or her soul.

And why would she even want to sleep with a man who had once owned her body and soul, then had betrayed her in the deepest, most profound way a man could betray a woman?

She smiled as Harriet sat down next to her. As usual the older lawyer was perfectly groomed, from the top of her shiny silver hair to the toes of her sensible black pumps.

"I didn't know you were a churchgoer," Harriet said.

"I'm not. I just came today because I was curious to see how everyone accepts Jerrod as the new minister on the block."

Harriet said nothing, but her pale-blue eyes held a knowing glint. Johnna scowled down at her hymnal, wishing she hadn't confided so much to her mentor. She couldn't fool Harriet, because Harriet knew too much about her.

Johnna wasn't sitting in church to see how the town would react to Jerrod. She was sitting here because she wanted to see Jerrod. She knew it, and she had a feeling Harriet knew it, as well.

The organ music swelled and the congregation rose to its feet as Jerrod entered through a side door and took his place at the pulpit. "Please join in the singing of our opening hymn," he said.

As the organ began to play and the church filled with the sound of voices raised in song, Johnna realized she'd decided to come here today for another reason besides just an opportunity to see Jerrod working.

There was a hole deep inside her, an ache of bereavement where her soul once had been. She wasn't sure where her soul had gone or what exactly was responsible for its absence. All she knew for certain was that someplace deep inside her, she'd awoken that morning knowing she wanted to come to church.

After the singing came to an end and everyone resumed their seats, Jerrod began his first sermon in the town that had once shunned him.

He was masterful. Energetic, strong and confident. His deep voice rang through the rafters as he talked about the joy of forgiveness. As his gaze lingered on her, she looked down at her hymnal.

It was easy to talk of forgiveness when you were the sinner and not the one sinned against, she thought. Easy to talk of forgiveness when it wasn't your heart that had been broken, your trust that had been betrayed, your life that had been destroyed.

She was grateful when the service was over. Seeing Jerrod so in command, so comfortable in his skin and so devastatingly handsome bothered her. And she didn't like it when she was bothered.

As the congregation filed out of the church, Jerrod stood at the door, shaking hands with each and every attendee. When he got to Johnna, he took her hand in the warmth of his, and she steeled herself against the heat that rose inside her from the contact.

"I'm glad to see you here," he said.

She shrugged and pulled her hand from his. "I figured I'd stop in and see you in action."

"Are you free for lunch?"

"No. I'm meeting Sam Clegg and George Kinnard. I'm interviewing them and they're supposed to finally be bringing me all the files on Tabitha

Warren's murder.'' Aware of the line of people behind her and that this wasn't the place to talk about a decade-old murder, she murmured a goodbye and moved on.

She stopped on the sidewalk, waiting for Harriet to join her. The two of them were meeting the deputies at Johnna's house.

''Good sermon,'' Harriet said as they walked to Johnna's car and Harriet's rental.

''It was all right,'' Johnna replied.

''He's a powerful presence behind the pulpit,'' Harriet observed.

He was a powerful presence anywhere, Johnna thought moments later as she drove to her house. He'd always radiated an energy—an edge of something unbridled, untamed, and he still possessed that quality.

And Johnna knew what it was like when that control cracked and his wild side was unleashed. She'd tasted that side of him in his kisses, knew the primal hunger she had once tapped inside him.

She shoved away those thoughts and, instead, focused on what she wanted to accomplish in the remainder of the day. She couldn't wait to get her hands on the Tabitha Warren file. Maybe, just maybe there would be something there to help in their defense of Erin.

Sheriff Broder had not been pleased at the request for the file. It had only been in the past six months that the Inferno Police Department was updating to computers, and most of the police files from years gone by were stuffed in boxes in the basement of the town hall.

He'd finally called her the night before to let her know they'd located the files. He knew she wanted to talk to the two deputies who initially responded to the Kramer house the night of Richard Kramer's murder, so he'd said he'd send the files with the two men this afternoon to her place.

She pulled into her driveway, aware of Harriet pulling in behind her. As she got out of her car, she spied her brother Luke across the street at Jerrod's place. Clad only in a pair of tight worn jeans, a carpenter belt riding low on his hips, he looked less like a workingman and more like a model for a sexy poster.

He was in the process of tearing out the porch. He paused long enough in his work to wave to her.

"This town seems to have an inordinate number of attractive young men," Harriet observed. "Too bad they all appear to be young enough to be my sons."

Johnna laughed. "That particular young man is one of my brothers. That's Luke, the family lady killer."

"Hmm, I can see why," Harriet replied as the two entered Johnna's house.

"How about some coffee?" Johnna asked as she led her friend into the kitchen and gestured her into a chair at the table.

"Sounds good."

Within minutes the two women were seated

across from each other at the table, coffee before them as they chattered about inconsequential things.

"This little hometown of yours is quite charming," Harriet said.

"It's a nice place," Johnna agreed. "There was a time I thought I hated it here, but when I was away for those years, I missed it desperately."

"It was important for you to come back here and face your demons."

Johnna grinned wryly. "You mean my father. He was the only demon in my life." Her smile slid away. "No matter how hard I tried, I could never make him love me."

"I think there are more demons here for you than just your father," Harriet said thoughtfully.

Before Johnna could ask her what she meant, a knock fell on her front door. "That must be Sam and George," she said as she rose.

Peering out her front window, she saw the patrol car parked in her driveway. She opened the door and greeted the two men who had obviously ridden together.

"Thank you for your time," she said as she led them through the living room and into the kitchen. "Coffee?" she asked after she'd introduced them to Harriet.

"No thanks," Sam said as he sat and placed several manila folders on the table before him. "The sheriff told us to make this as quick as possible. Both of us are supposed to be on duty."

"I promise this won't take long," Johnna said as

once again she sat down at the table. "As I'm sure you both know, Harriet and I are representing Erin Kramer in her defense. According to Erin, both of you, at various times, have responded to domestic-dispute problems at the Kramer residence. What I would like to know is why there are no official records indicating that Richard Kramer was beating the hell out of his wife."

George raked a hand through his thinning gray hair and eyed her with more than a touch of irritation. "That sounds more like an accusation than a question."

Johnna shrugged. "It wasn't intended as an accusation—unless you have something to feel guilty about."

"Whoa now," Sam exclaimed, and held up his hands in mock surrender. "Let's not get all worked up here." His pale-blue eyes held Johnna's gaze. "I'd say I responded to the Kramer household more than anyone else on the force. You've probably heard that me and Richard were friends, but that doesn't mean I didn't try to do my job."

"What do you mean?" Harriet asked as she pulled a pad and pen from her oversize purse.

He shrugged. "I knew Richard had a drinking problem, and I knew he could be a mean, ugly drunk. Most of the time when I went out to the Kramer place, it was just after he and Erin had gone a round. I told Erin over and over again that things wouldn't change unless she pressed charges against him or made him get help, but she refused. And she always begged me not to make an official report. Besides, I never saw any physical injuries on her.''

"Same with me," George explained. "I went out there a couple of times and found them screaming and yelling at each other, throwing things and huffing and puffing, but they always seemed to cool down after a little talk.''

"Then how do you explain the hospital records that show all kinds of bumps and bruises and broken bones on Erin?" Johnna asked.

Sam stared down at the table, and when he met Johnna's gaze once again, his eyes were filled with regret. "Look, Johnna, if any of us had known how bad things really were between Erin and Richard, maybe we would have handled things differently. Hell, I figured eventually she'd leave his sorry ass, but I never thought she'd kill him.''

"She didn't," Johnna said.

"There isn't any evidence pointing to anyone else," George put in.

"And now there's the matter of the prenuptial agreement," Sam added.

"Prenuptial agreement?" Johnna looked at Sam sharply. "I haven't heard anything about a prenup.''

"We just got wind of it ourselves this morning. Richard's lawyer has been on a cruise for the past week. He got back in town this morning, heard about Richard and contacted Sheriff Broder and Chet Maxwell.''

"Let me guess, if she divorced him, she would have walked away with nothing," Johnna said flatly.

"You got it," Sam replied.

"Divorced she gets nothing. Dead she gets not only all his wealth, but also a cool million-dollar insurance policy," George added.

"You know what they say—follow the money and you find your motive," Sam said.

Johnna sighed. "Got any more bad news?"

"Nope."

For the next few minutes Johnna and Harriet asked questions of the two men who had been the initial responders to Erin's emergency call on the night of the murder.

When Johnna had asked everything she felt she needed to about the murder scene, she looked at Harriet to see if her colleague had any more questions.

"I guess that does it for now," Harriet said.

"Then we'd better hit the road," George said as he rose from the chair.

"Here are the files Sheriff Broder said we should give you." Sam tapped the manila folders with a knuckle as he stood. "How come you wanted the files on Tabitha Warren's murder?"

"Curiosity," Johnna replied. "Were either of you involved in that investigation?"

"Tabitha Warren?" George frowned.

"Nine years ago," Sam explained. "I remember because I was a rookie. It was my first look at murder."

"Ah, over at the trailer park. That murder was

never solved, was it?'' George's eyes widened. ''Now I remember—she was Erin's mother.''

''Yeah, that's right,'' Sam agreed. His pale eyes seemed to grow paler. ''I'll never forget how Erin looked that night…covered with her mother's blood and screaming.'' He shook his head. ''Apparently when she found her mother's body, she tried to…tried to hold Tabitha's head together until help could arrive.''

Johnna's heart ached with the image of Erin trying to save a mother who was already dead. She empathized with the young girl who had been the first to discover her mother's body. She wished Sam had never shared that bit of information. She didn't want to feel any emotion where Erin was concerned.

''If I remember right, speculation at the time was that Tabitha had picked up some drifter at the Honky Tonk that night and he murdered her, then left town. Tabitha had a reputation for being pretty loose and wild,'' George said as they left the kitchen and headed for the front door.

''I can't believe we've just now discovered a damn prenuptial,'' Johnna said a moment later as she stalked back into the kitchen and paced the floor in short, staccato footsteps.

''Prenuptials are fairly common these days,'' Harriet said. ''I'm sure we can spin it enough to take the sting out of it.'' Harriet finished her coffee, then stood.

''I hope so,'' Johnna replied. ''Because if we can't, that information is damning.''

"I'll head back to the bed-and-breakfast and have a little talk with Erin, explain to her that we don't like surprises."

"And I'm going to spend the afternoon reading this file on Tabitha Warren's murder," Johnna said.

"You think you'll find a connection?"

"I don't know. I just can't figure out why Richard would have clippings about a murder that occurred years before he even moved to Inferno."

Harriet smiled at Johnna. "You know as well as I do that people can be ghoulish." Her smile fell aside and she gazed at Johnna curiously. "Do you remember the murder?"

"Vaguely," Johnna replied as the two women left the kitchen and headed toward the front door. "I remember hearing that somebody had been murdered at the trailer park, but it seemed far removed from me and my life. Jerrod and I had broken up and he'd left Inferno. As much as I hate to admit it, at that time in my life I was far too absorbed in my own heartaches to think about what was going on around me."

Harriet smiled and patted Johnna's arm. "Don't be too hard on yourself. Most teenagers are incredibly self-absorbed, and I am witness to the fact that you've grown marvelously well since then."

Johnna laughed, gave her friend a hug, then the two said their goodbyes and Harriet left. Johnna went directly into her bedroom and changed out of the suit she'd worn to church, eager to get out of the heels and hose.

Moments later, clad in a short terry-cloth robe, she grabbed the files and curled up on the sofa. She'd worked her hours at the ranch for the week already, anticipating an unusually leisurely Sunday afternoon today and an early night to bed.

With only two weeks before Erin's trial began, she suspected these would be the last hours of leisure for some time to come.

It didn't take long for her to get through the file Sam and George had brought. Unfortunately there was not a lot of information there. The investigation into Tabitha Warren's murder had been perfunctory at best.

There was the medical examiner's report, a drawing of the crime scene and several photographs, but no reports of interviews, statements from neighbors or anything to indicate that anyone had much cared that a woman had been brutally beaten to death.

However, what truly bothered her was that there was absolutely nothing to explain why Richard Kramer had kept clippings from the murder.

Had he kept them simply out of some perverse curiosity? Certainly if Johnna had married a man whose mother had been murdered, she would have had a certain amount of interest in the case. But as she'd mentioned to Jerrod earlier, reading clippings in the local library could have sated that interest.

She carried the files into the back bedroom, which she used as a home office, and set them on the desk. She wasn't sure what she'd been looking for, but knew she hadn't found it.

She left the office and wandered back into the living room and to the front window. Peeking out, she saw Jerrod, clad only in a pair of jeans, working alongside Luke on building a new front porch.

Even through the glass of her window she could hear the sounds of the two men talking and laughing together.

A sigh escaped her as her gaze played over Jerrod's bare back, the sinewy muscle that rippled as he lifted a piece of wood. Her fingers tingled with the tactile memory of what those muscles felt like, and a dull ache began to throb deep inside her.

Her mind spun with bittersweet images of what might have been...what should have been. They were supposed to have shared a future together. They had planned all the details of the house where they would live and the number of children they would have. They were supposed to have stayed in love forever.

From the moment she had met Jerrod she'd believed that fate had delivered him to her as a reward for all the hurt, all the pain, all the heartache she had endured from her father. Jerrod was to have been her destiny, and she'd always felt as if their love had been preordained.

She whirled away from the window, refusing to dwell on what might have been. The fact of the matter was that Jerrod had ruined everything, that he obviously hadn't loved her the same way she had loved him. And there was no going back.

She returned to her office and reread all the information she had about Richard Kramer's murder, taking notes and outlining an opening statement. Darkness had fallen outside when she finally pulled herself from her work. Realizing she hadn't eaten all day, she went into the kitchen, made herself a sandwich, then sat at the table and ate.

It was still difficult for her to believe that the edgy young man who had stolen her heart, the young man with wildness in his soul and a glint of danger in his eyes was now a minister.

And he still stirred her. Where before it had been that edge of wildness that had pulled her to him, now it was the sense of inner peace that radiated from him that she found so magnetic.

She finished her sandwich and decided to call it a night. Tomorrow she was meeting with Judd Stevens, the private eye she'd hired to do investigative work for her. Tomorrow also heralded the beginning of a new week, and the twenty-five hours she would have to put in at the ranch.

Frowning, she thought of how tense things had been between her and her brother Matthew. She and Luke had always been the closest of the Delaney siblings, but it was her eldest brother she wished she could connect with in some sort of positive way. And it was Matthew who seemed the most distant and disapproving of all her siblings.

Minutes later as she crawled into bed, she consciously shoved all thoughts of Jerrod, her dysfunctional family and the murder crimes aside, seeking the sweet peace of sleep.

*   *   *

She didn't know what woke her, but one minute she was dreaming and the next she was wide-awake, her heart pounding.

Not moving anything but her head, she looked at her clock, surprised to see that it was almost midnight. Had it been a dream that had rocketed her awake? A nightmare? She didn't remember dreaming anything.

And then she heard it—the distinctive creak of a floorboard. At the same time a flash of light swept past her darkened bedroom doorway.

Someone's in my house! The words screamed in her head. And whoever it was didn't belong here. Terror shot through her.

She sat up, uncertain what to do. The phone! Her first impulse was to reach for it and call for help.

Trying desperately not to make a sound, not to even breathe, she reached out for the phone on her nightstand—and the glass of water she kept there crashed to the floor.

Instantly, a dark form filled her doorway. The bright beam from a flashlight blinded her as she struggled to get out of bed. Before she could free her legs from the sheets, the flashlight slammed her on the side of her head.

Brilliant starbursts exploded behind her eyes, and she fell back against the pillows as pain ripped through her.

Within moments the pain had ebbed enough for her to know she was in the house alone. Whoever had attacked her was gone.

She half fell from her bed, then lurched down the hallway. Straight ahead the front door stood open, the starry night sky visible.

Weak-kneed and nauseous, she stumbled outside, and it was only then that she cried out for help.

Jerrod sat on a folding lawn chair where the new front porch would eventually be completed. Night had fallen hours earlier, and he knew he should be in bed, but it had been a busy day and winding down seemed impossible.

He had been both surprised and inordinately pleased to look out over the congregation that morning and see Johnna sitting in one of the back pews.

He'd also been pleased by the warmth and acceptance he'd felt from everyone who had attended his service. It appeared, at least on the surface, that the good people of Inferno had forgiven him his past transgressions, and he, in turn, had forgiven them.

However, he knew that the one person whose forgiveness he most wanted remained unmoved in her heart. Johnna. He took a sip of his coffee, his gaze lingering on the house across the street.

He'd had years to think about that night with Erin, to play and replay the events that had occurred, to wonder what he might have done differently. He'd had years to mourn what had been lost, what price he'd paid because he'd been young and immature, and overwhelmed with the circumstances of the moment.

As he stared at the house, the front door flew open

and a dark figure ran out, instantly disappearing into the shadows between the houses.

Jerrod stood, his coffee cup falling to the ground. Before he could take any action, Johnna appeared at the front door, a faint cry escaping her lips.

He raced across the lawns, his heart in his throat as Johnna clung to her porch railing as if by letting go she would fall to the ground.

"Johnna," he cried as he reached her. "Are you all right?"

"Oh, Jerrod, I..." Her voice was faint and she released her hold on the railing in exchange for him.

She clung to him, her entire body trembling. "Somebody was here. Somebody was in my house." She kept her face buried in the front of his shirt, and within seconds, his shirt felt wet and he realized she must be crying.

"But are you all right?" he asked, holding her tightly against him. She nodded and he guided her toward the front door. "Come on, let's go inside."

She released her hold on him and took a step back. He gasped as he realized what he'd thought was the moisture of tears was actually blood dripping from a wound at her hairline.

Her eyes widened as she stared at the front of his shirt. She reached up and touched her head, a deep moan escaping her lips.

He led her to the sofa. "Sit here and let me get a wet cloth." He left her there and hurried to the bathroom, where he grabbed a washcloth, wet it, then raced back to her.

"Tell me what happened," he said as he sat next to her and began to dab at the wound.

"I woke up and somebody was in the house." She winced and bit her lower lip, then continued, "I reached for the phone on my nightstand, but I knocked over a glass of water. He must have heard me and he ran into my bedroom and whacked me on the head."

"We need to call the sheriff," Jerrod said, reluctant to move away from her. He wanted to gather her into his arms and hold her close. Although the wound to her head didn't appear to be too bad, the shivering of her body and the fear that darkened her eyes worried him.

He handed her the cloth and gestured for her to continue to press it against her head, then reached for the phone on the end table. He punched in the numbers for the sheriff's office and spoke to the deputy on desk duty.

"Sheriff Broder should be here in just a few minutes," he said as he hung up. Then he went into her bathroom to get her some aspirin and a glass of water. "Should I call for a doctor?" he asked.

She shook her head, her eyes huge as she swallowed the medicine. "I think I'm fine. The aspirin should help. Does it look bad?" She removed the cloth and leaned toward him.

"I don't think you need stitches or anything. The bleeding is slowing." Again he fought the impulse to pull her close, keep her safe and secure in his arms.

He'd never seen her look so small, so vulnerable.

Clad only in a long nightshirt, her eyes so dark they were nearly black, she looked younger and more defenseless than ever.

Within minutes Sheriff Jeffrey Broder had arrived and took first her statement, then Jerrod's. Neither of them could give many details about the intruder other than, judging from height and body type, it was a male.

They discovered that he must have gotten in through the window of the empty spare room. Johnna couldn't remember whether the window had been locked. Broder ordered a deputy with a fingerprint kit to dust the window.

While the deputy was busy doing that, Broder walked with Jerrod and Johnna through the house so she could see if anything had been stolen. She could find nothing missing.

"You must have disturbed him before he got started," Broder said. They were back in the living room, Johnna seated on the sofa and the two men standing nearby.

"Maybe," she replied. "Or maybe it wasn't a burglary at all."

"What do you mean?" Jerrod asked.

She shrugged. "I don't know…maybe he came in here to hit me over the head—or worse."

"Johnna, you aren't making sense," Broder exclaimed. "Why would anyone break into your house just to hurt you?"

"Why would anyone spray paint on my car and leave a warning note there?" she countered.

"You think this is about Erin's case?" Jerrod frowned thoughtfully.

Johnna sighed. "I don't know what to think."

At that moment the deputy returned. "Whoever opened that window had gloves on," he said. "There wasn't a print anywhere to be found."

"Just my luck, a smart goon," Johnna said.

"I'll do what I can to find out who's responsible, but I've got to be honest with you, Johnna. Without prints or any kind of physical evidence, it's going to be hard," Broder said.

"I know, Jeff. I don't expect miracles." She stood to walk with him to her door. "And from now on when I close my eyes at night to sleep, I'll make sure the doors and windows are locked up tight."

"I hate to think we've come to that in Inferno, but I guess we have," Jeffrey replied, then said his goodbyes, and he and his deputy left.

Johnna returned to the sofa, where she sat and pulled her legs up beneath her. There were still dark shadows in her eyes, and Jerrod didn't know whether it was fear or exhaustion that pulled her features taut.

"Maybe I should get out of here and let you go back to bed," he said softly.

Her eyes flared wide in obvious panic. "No, please don't go yet." She patted the sofa next to her. "Sit with me for a few minutes." Her gaze held such appeal he realized she wasn't ready to be alone in the house.

He sat down next to her and this time didn't fight his impulse to pull her close. She came willingly, her arms curling around his neck as she lay her head on his shoulder.

"I was so scared," she murmured. "I've never known what terror was until I opened my eyes and realized I wasn't alone in the house." A shiver accompanied her words.

"Shh. You're safe now," he returned, stroking her slender back as a fierce protectiveness filled him.

She was so independent, so strong-willed. This momentary neediness merely spoke of the depth of the trauma she'd just suffered.

The minutes of the dark night ticked by and still he held her close. In the intimacy of their embrace, he felt the stir of desire. Her nearness provoked a river of heat inside him, the scent of her, floral and feminine, electrifying every nerve ending in his body.

He fought it, as he'd fought it for all the years he'd been away from her. He tried not to notice the sweet, clean smell of her hair, the press of her breasts against his side, the heat from her body that made him think of naked skin and heady release.

She raised her head and gazed at him as if she could feel his inner battle. The fear that had darkened her eyes for most of the night was gone, replaced by smoldering flames he felt inside his very soul.

She didn't say a word, but rather leaned up and touched her lips to his. The kiss was nothing more than a mere meeting of mouths, but it was enough to set him afire.

It was she who led the way, deepening the kiss

by touching the tip of his tongue with hers. Aware of her vulnerable state, he accepted rather than initiated, trying desperately to maintain control and take only what she offered.

Control, he told himself. He must maintain control. He did not want to do anything that would serve to put distance between them when the dawn of a new day arrived.

As the kiss lingered, deepening in intensity, she molded her body to his. He could feel her heartbeat thundering, and his own answering with a frantic beat.

When she finally drew away from him and stood, she didn't say a word, just took him by the hand and pulled him up from the sofa.

Still clutching her hand, she led him down the hallway and into her bedroom, where the light was off but moonlight spilled in through the window.

She released his hand, peeled off the robe she'd put on before the sheriff had arrived, then pulled the nightshirt over her head, leaving her wearing only a pair of white bikini panties. She slid beneath the sheets and gestured for him to join her there.

His control snapped as he realized fate was giving him a second chance with the woman who'd never, ever been completely out of his heart.

Chapter 8

Johnna didn't want to think about right or wrong, consequences or repercussions. All she knew was she wanted Jerrod.

She wanted him in bed next to her, wanted his body close to hers through the remaining dark hours of the night. She wanted his kisses and his caresses to banish the cold fear that still knotted in the pit of her stomach.

As she watched, he took off his shirt and jeans, leaving him clad in only a pair of briefs. Her breath caught in her chest as he removed those, as well, leaving him beautifully naked to her hungry gaze.

Physically he'd changed little from the taut, well-built young man he had been. His shoulders were still impossibly broad, his waist and hips still lean.

His muscular legs were well shaped, and there was no mistaking the fact that he was fully aroused.

As he slid into bed next to her, she kicked off her panties, not wanting any barrier at all between their naked skin.

When he took her into his arms, their bodies breast to chest, hip to hip, she felt a sweet homecoming. Her body conformed to his in a memory of familiarity. It was as if not only her head remembered the feel of his body against hers, but as if every cell of her skin and nerves had also retained the memory.

When they kissed again, she tasted his edgy wildness and his ravenous hunger, a hunger she met with her own.

As they kissed, his hands cupped her breasts. His thumbs raked over her hardened nipples and shot spirals of pleasure through her.

She ran her hands across his broad back, loving the way his warm skin and the underlying hard muscle felt beneath her fingertips.

As their kiss lingered and his hands stroked fever into her skin, the icy fear that had gripped her melted away, unable to sustain itself as she fell into the magic of his caresses.

He tore his mouth from hers, his breathing ragged and sharp. He moved his lips across her cheek, then nibbled on the sensitive skin just behind her ear. Waves of heat swept through her, sexual heat she had not felt for so long.

She had not been with a man since Jerrod had left

Inferno all those years ago. He had been her first lover. He had been her only lover.

As his mouth continued to nip and tease the skin near her ear, one of his hands moved downward, lingering for a moment on her hip, then touching her intimately.

She gasped in sheer pleasure and arched her body to meet his touch. At the same time, she wrapped her fingers around him and heard his moan of pleasure.

She stoked her fingers up and down the length of him, but with a small cry he shoved her hand away. In the moonlit room, his gaze bore into hers. "Sweet Johnna, you can't touch me. I have no control..."

And she loved that he was already at the place where a simple touch of her hand could drive him over the edge. However, the thought lingered only a moment, then was banished as his intimate touch sent her head spinning and made conscious thought impossible.

It was as if he'd never been parted from her, as if he knew her as intimately as anyone ever could. He knew just where to touch and with how much pressure to give her the maximum pleasure. And it wasn't long before she was spiraling out of control and shattering into a million pieces.

Before she'd recovered, before she even drew a breath, he entered her, taking her with command, possessing her with mastery.

Years melted away and she was once again eighteen and loving Jerrod. She locked her legs around his waist, deepening his penetration and wanting to hold him there forever, trap him against her, inside her.

His mouth devoured hers and she returned his kisses with her own savage hunger. "Johnna, Johnna," he breathed into her mouth, and although she'd always hated her name, she loved the way it sounded falling from his lips.

Speech for her was impossible as she felt herself climbing higher and higher, felt him pulsing deep inside her and his heart racing against her own.

Then she was tumbling over the precipice. She cried out his name as he stiffened against her, moaning low and deep as release came.

For long moments afterward they remained entwined, their breaths coming more slowly and their heartbeats returning to a more normal pace.

Johnna was the first one to move. She unlocked her legs from around him, then he rolled to his side and brought her tightly against him.

She knew she should get up, distance herself from the postcoital cuddle. With desire sated, rational thought returned and she knew she should send him home. What they had just shared had been inevitable, but it had nothing to do with reality—or tomorrow.

However, in all the times in the distant past she and Jerrod had made love, they had never shared an entire night together. Always before, they'd made love, then parted to return to their homes before their disappearance was discovered.

As his body warmth surrounded her and his breath whispered against her hair, she closed her eyes and dreamed of second chances.

She awakened slowly, instantly aware that she was still held in Jerrod's embrace and appalled that the sunshine flooding in through the windows was the light of midmorning.

In the glare of that light, all dreams of second chances faded, leaving only the bittersweet taste of what might have been in her mouth.

She could give Jerrod her time, could even give him her body, but he would never, ever get a second chance to get into her heart.

Besides, she didn't have a heart. It had been broken into a million pieces on the day her baby had died, and those pieces had disappeared on the wind that blew the day she buried little Miranda.

Jerrod was still asleep when she gently untangled herself from him and left the bed. Quietly as possible, she gathered her clothes for the day, then went into the bathroom and stared at her reflection in the mirror. She looked like hell.

Her short hair was standing on end and dried blood clung to the cut at her hairline. But it was her eyes that bothered her the most. They glowed. They sparkled. They looked like the eyes of a woman who loved—who was loved.

"Lies," she whispered to her reflection, then turned the water on in the shower. Moments later she stood beneath a hot spray, scrubbing off the memory of his touch, any scent of him that might linger on her skin.

Last night had been a mistake. The break-in had left her frightened. She'd been weak and vulnerable and had allowed Jerrod far too close. She didn't intend for it to happen again. She couldn't let it happen again.

By the time she had showered and dressed, Jerrod was no longer in her bed, and the scent of freshly brewed coffee filled the air.

He stood leaning with his back against the counter in the kitchen. Clad only in his jeans, his feet bare and his hair tousled from sleep, he looked deliciously handsome and far too much at home.

"Good morning," he greeted her, his eyes warm and intimate. "Did you sleep well?"

"Fine," she said briskly. "But I'm running late." She picked up her purse and her car keys. "You can lock up when you're finished here."

"Don't you even have time for a quick cup of coffee?" he asked, a frown creasing his forehead.

"Not this morning. I was supposed to meet with Judd Stevens fifteen minutes ago. He'll be waiting for me at my office."

"What about lunch? Can we meet somewhere?"

"Sorry, I'm going to be pretty busy all day." She felt his gaze on her, but refused to look at him. Distance—she desperately needed it to feel safe. "We'll catch up with each other later." With these words she left the kitchen and hurried out of the house.

Seeing him half-naked in her kitchen sipping coffee had felt almost as intimate as what they'd shared in the dark of the night. Regret tainted the memories of the night before. She'd always known he'd been a wonderful lover, but there was no place for him in her life now.

She'd never been able to connect with her father. Other than a rather superficial one with Luke, she had almost no relationship with her brothers. She was better off alone, depending on nobody.

Yet, as she drove from her house to her office, she wanted to weep...because making love to Jerrod had been better than she'd remembered.

There had been no awkward fumbling, no tentative caresses. He'd played her body like a maestro with a treasured instrument. He'd sent sweet music ringing through her, music she hadn't heard for many years.

Even now, her body still felt the imprint of each and every one of his touches. Her lips still held the imprint of his. He was knocking on the door of her heart, but she refused to let him in.

She'd let him in once, and the result had been pain greater than anything she'd ever known. She'd learned her lesson well where Jerrod was concerned.

As she pulled up in front of her law office, she saw Judd Stevens sitting on the bench outside. Judd was a big, handsome man with dark hair gone prematurely gray at the temples. He had sharp green eyes and strong, defined facial features.

She knew little about him, only that he had once been an FBI agent and had moved to Inferno two years earlier, and worked cases around the country as a private investigator.

Why couldn't she feel something for him? He was single, extremely attractive and gainfully employed. But no bells rang, no sparks ignited when she was around him. Chemistry only seemed to work with the one man she didn't want in her life, with the one man who had betrayed her.

"Sorry I'm late," she said as she got out of her car and approached him.

He stood and nodded. "It's all right. I was just sitting here going over my notes in my head."

She unlocked the front door and ushered him through the small reception area and into her private office. He sat in the chair before her desk and withdrew a small notepad from his shirt pocket.

She sat behind her desk and looked at him expectantly. "I hope you have some good news for me," she said.

"I've got news, but I'm not sure how good you'll think it is," he said.

Johnna got legal pad and pen ready. "Let me have it," she said.

Judd leaned back in the chair. "There's something peculiar about the Kramer finances."

"What do you mean?"

"According to the records I examined, Richard Kramer was making cash deposits of five hundred dollars a month into his personal account for the past two years."

Johnna frowned. "Embezzlement?"

"Doesn't appear to be. His business records were meticulously kept, no discrepancies."

"So where is the money coming from each month?"

"Maybe blackmail?" Judd raised a dark eyebrow.

"Blackmail? Kramer was blackmailing somebody?" Johnna's head spun as she frantically took notes on the legal pad.

"I'm just speculating. Five hundred dollars isn't an enormous amount of money, but added up every month for two years, it's a fair sum. But this is the part I don't think you're going to be very happy about," he continued. "Did you know that your client was having an affair with Dale Jenkins?"

"What? You mean, Dale Jenkins, the mayor of Inferno—that Dale Jenkins?" Johnna's pen slid from her fingers as she stared at Judd. "Please tell me you're kidding."

"I assume by your expression that your client hasn't mentioned this," he said.

"No. I'm sure she knew it would be incriminating where motive was concerned." Anger raged through Johnna. She didn't like surprises, especially ones of such magnitude that came to light from a source other than her client.

"It appears the mayor and Erin were meeting occasionally at the Blue Bird Inn, just outside of town. They were very discreet."

"If they were so discreet, how did you find out about it?"

He smiled. "Money is a great motivator to loosen

tongues. Erin's housekeeper apparently knew more about the lady she worked for than how she liked her furniture polished.''

Johnna sighed. She finished her interview with Judd, then left her office. She needed to see Erin, wanted to confront her about this latest tidbit of information, but first she wanted to go by her own place and go through all the interviews she'd had with Erin. Then she intended to see Jerrod and learn if he'd known about Erin's affair.

Besides, it might be a good idea to take Jerrod with her to see Erin, she thought. Perhaps he could keep her from killing her own client.

The break-in, making love to Jerrod, all that seemed like ancient history as she wondered if perhaps she was defending a guilty woman.

Jerrod and Luke sat on Jerrod's half-finished front porch, taking a break. Luke had arrived two hours earlier sporting a deadly hangover and had instantly popped the top of a beer he'd brought with him.

''Hair of the dog,'' he explained as he got to work.

Jerrod said nothing, although he wondered what demons drove a handsome, capable young man like Luke to drink so much and play at life.

He had a feeling Adam Delaney had managed to scar each and every one of his children with his physical, verbal and mental abuse. He also had a feeling there was a particular chamber in hell for men like Adam Delaney who abused the innocent souls of their children.

Both men looked up as Johnna's car sped down the street and squealed into her driveway. She flew out of the car and into her house, the slam of her front door echoing through the quiet of the neighborhood.

"Whew, looks like somebody shot a burr under her saddle," Luke exclaimed, and reached for another beer from the six-pack he'd brought with him.

Jerrod said nothing. He wasn't at all sure that he wasn't the burr under her saddle. The night before he'd stayed awake long after she'd fallen asleep, treasuring those moments when she'd clung to him in need, in vulnerable openness.

And for those sweet minutes, he'd felt as if nothing had changed between them, as if they were still young and crazy in love and facing a future as bright as the Inferno sun. For those precious moments he'd forgotten how badly he'd once hurt her and the barriers she'd erected against him.

However, morning brought reality and she made it quite clear to him that even though they had spent the night in each other's arms, making love with abandon, nothing had really changed between them.

The distance between them that morning had been a chasm he'd had no idea how to breach. He'd wanted to reach for her, to draw her against him and hold her, but he'd been afraid it'd only serve to push her farther away.

At the moment he didn't need to worry about distance. Her front door swung open and she marched out, heading in his direction, her pretty features twisted into a mask of suppressed anger.

He and Luke both stood as she stopped in front of them. "Hey, sis," Luke said easily.

"You drink too much," she snapped, then turned to Jerrod. "Did you know that Erin was having an affair with Dale Jenkins?"

"Who's Dale Jenkins?" he asked.

"The mayor of this good town," Luke replied, and tipped his beer can to his lips as if in deliberate defiance of Johnna's comment about his drinking.

"And Erin was having an affair with him?" Jerrod said in surprise.

"According to my private investigator, she was. I'm on my way over to talk to her now. You want to come along to make sure I don't kill her?"

Although the invitation for him to join her was hardly given graciously, Jerrod jumped at the opportunity to spend time with her and try to breach the distance she'd put between them that morning.

"Okay, I'll ride along." He looked at Luke. "You'll be all right by yourself?"

"Sure. I appreciate the help you've given me this morning," Luke replied easily. "And maybe you should take up a little drinking, sis. It'll do wonders for your stress level."

Johnna didn't rise to the bait, but instead, whirled on her heel and headed back to her car. Jerrod said a quick goodbye to Luke, then hurried after her.

She didn't speak as they left her driveway and

drove to the bed-and-breakfast where Erin was staying. Finally it was Jerrod who broke the silence.

"Are you sure your information about Erin and the mayor is correct?" he asked, although this was the last thing he wanted to talk about. What he wanted to talk about was last night. He wanted to tell her how right it had felt to have her in his arms, how the magic was still there for him.

But one look at her face told him she wasn't in any mood to hear about magic.

"Judd Stevens is a good investigator. He wouldn't have told me this if he didn't have substantial evidence to back it up," she replied, her voice filled with tension.

She slapped a palm against the steering wheel. "I can't believe Erin wouldn't have told me this. I told her from the very beginning, no secrets. I told her I needed to know absolutely everything about her, her life with Richard and anything else that might be important in defending her. An affair," she scoffed irritably. "Can't anyone be faithful in this world?"

Although he knew she was talking about Erin and this latest discovery, her words struck Jerrod like pointed barbs. He wanted—needed—to explain to her the events of the night of his betrayal of her and wondered if she'd ever give him a chance to explain.

"If this is true and Chet Maxwell gets hold of this information, Erin is finished. He'll beat it to death as a motive for Richard's murder. Erin kills Richard and she not only gets Richard's wealth, but is free to be with the man she's cheating with."

Jerrod nodded. "Have you also realized that if Erin was having an affair with this Dale Jenkins, then you have another suspect to point a finger at?"

He watched the play of emotions on her face, wondering if she had any idea how beautiful she was. She was no fragile beauty; rather, her features were bold and strong, and her face held character.

She pulled to the curb in front of the bed-and-breakfast. "Dale loved Erin, but Richard stood in the way of their happiness, so Dale murdered Richard." She nodded. "I don't believe it, but I can argue it to muddy the waters."

"Why don't you believe it?"

She shut off the engine and turned to look at him. "It's obvious you haven't met our young, dapper mayor. He would never be involved in anything that might muss his hair." Her lips curved up in a wry grin. "In fact, I'm shocked to think that he actually indulges in sex. He probably wears a hairnet during the act."

Jerrod laughed, aware that in the space of the last few minutes some of the ice between them had melted.

She raked a hand through her short hair. "Well, let's go inside and see what Erin has to say about all this. If we're lucky, Judd Stevens is wrong."

Judd Stevens wasn't wrong. Minutes later Erin tearfully confessed to Johnna, Jerrod and Harriet that it was true. She was involved with the mayor and had been involved with him for some time.

"Why didn't you tell us this from the very beginning?'' Johnna demanded as she paced in front of the chair where Erin sat sobbing.

''Because I love Dale. Because I didn't want to drag him through this...this mess. He's going to be up for reelection, and how is it going to look if people find out he was not only having an affair, but having an affair with somebody like me?'' Her words came between sobs.

Harriet placed a hand on Erin's shoulder. ''What do you mean, dear, somebody like you?''

Jerrod knew what she meant. He'd once felt the same way, felt the burden of where he lived and how the town saw him.

''I'm nothing but trailer trash!'' Erin cried. ''And no matter what I do or what happens, I'll always be just trailer trash. That's why I didn't want anyone to know Richard beat me.'' The words tumbled from her, forced out by a pain too enormous to bear.

''Oh, Erin,'' Johnna said softly.

''What do you expect from trailer trash?'' she continued bitterly. ''Everyone knows we sleep around and get beat up. We drink too much and act cheap. I know what everyone is saying—that poor Richard tried to lift me up out of the gutter and look what I did to him in return.''

She drew a deep breath and swiped at her tears. ''I didn't tell you about Dale because he is the one good thing I've ever had in my life. I didn't want that ruined, and I didn't want him to bear the brunt of people knowing he was dating trailer trash.''

Jerrod glanced at Johnna, wondering if she was

remembering the night she'd called him "nothing but trailer trash," if she had any idea how deeply those words had cut.

"Did Richard know you were having an affair?" Johnna asked.

Erin's eyes widened. "Absolutely not. If he had known, he would have killed Dale…or me…or both of us. Richard didn't have a clue."

"Did Dale know that Richard beat you?" Jerrod asked.

"No." Erin looked down at her clenched hands in her lap. "I never told him, and when I had bruises or whatever, I didn't see Dale until I was healed. I didn't want him to know. I didn't want anyone to know."

"Do you know anything about five-hundred-dollar cash deposits Richard was making each month into his personal account?" Johnna asked. "The deposits began about two years ago, and one was made a week before his death."

"I didn't know anything about his finances," Erin explained. "Richard gave me a small allowance to buy groceries, but that was it."

"Why didn't you just leave him?" Johnna asked, her irritation with Erin still evident in the tautness of her features, in the sharp edge in her voice.

Again Erin looked down at her hands. "Because I was afraid," she said softly. "And because he told me nobody else would ever want me, that he'd picked me out of the gutter and I'd be back in the gutter if it wasn't for him." She looked up, her eyes dark with pain. "Richard convinced me that I didn't deserve anything better."

Jerrod's heart ached with his friend's pain. She'd been a young girl scorned by a town, a young girl whose mother's murder had been written off as nothing important, and Erin had continued that pain by marrying a man who played on her vulnerabilities.

Again he looked at Johnna, wondering if she remained unmoved by Erin's words or if she realized that while the town's attitude toward Erin and the circumstances of her upbringing had scarred her, Johnna's father had scarred her in the same way.

He just wasn't sure he was the man who could heal her scars and make her whole.

Chapter 9

Johnna didn't want to be emotionally touched by Erin. She wanted, needed, to keep herself distant, but it was impossible not to be touched.

Erin had been a victim all her life, a victim of a drunk and careless mother, the victim of a town's and then a husband's cruelty.

"Johnna, could I speak to you alone?" Erin asked.

Johnna frowned. "Harriet is my co-counsel in your defense. Jerrod is your friend and is helping with the case. We have no secrets here."

"Please," Erin said, her eyes begging.

Harriet grabbed Jerrod's arm. "I'll just take this handsome hunk down to the dining room and get us some coffee."

Before Johnna could protest, the two left the room

and closed the door behind them. Johnna sank onto the edge of the bed, facing Erin. "Please, don't tell me you have more secrets to confess."

Erin shook her head. "No, but what I want to talk to you about is just between you and me. I want to talk about the night of my mother's murder."

Johnna nodded, instant adrenaline flooding through her. "What about it?"

Erin stood and walked to the window, her back to Johnna as she spoke. "I loved my mother, but I was ashamed of her. I didn't understand why she could never hold a job or why we had to live in that horrid place. I knew how the men in town thought of her, and they were right. She was easy and drank way too much."

"Do you know if, at that time, she was seeing anyone in particular?" Johnna asked.

Erin turned to face her. "She never saw anyone in particular. Whoever had the price of a couple of drinks was Mom's boyfriend of the moment." The pain of a lost child was evident on her face.

"But that's not what I want to talk about." She returned to her chair and once again gazed at Johnna. "What I need to tell you is what happened that night between me and Jerrod. That night is when we both betrayed you."

Rebellion rose inside Johnna at the same time her mind worked to accept what Erin had just said. That night? The very night of Erin's mother's murder? Johnna had never realized that was when Jerrod had betrayed her.

It doesn't make any difference, she told herself, embracing the old anger that now felt as comfortable as an old worn bathrobe. It doesn't matter what was going on that night. He cheated on me, and that's all that matters.

She stood, wanting to run, wanting to escape. "Erin, I really don't think we need to—"

"Yes, we do," Erin interrupted with uncharacteristic forcefulness. "Maybe you don't need to hear about it, but I need to tell you about it. For all these years I've felt so guilty about you and Jerrod, and I need to explain to you what happened."

"You shouldn't have felt guilty..." Johnna's voice trailed off uneasily. She didn't want to talk about this.

"Of course I should have felt guilty," Erin countered. "I knew how you felt about Jerrod...and I knew how he felt about you." She leaned her head back against the chair and closed her eyes, pain twisting her delicate features. "But that night everything went so crazy." Her eyes opened and she gazed at Johnna intently. "I went a little bit crazy," she said.

Again she rose from her chair as if finding the sedentary act of sitting impossible. "From the moment I found my mother's body in the middle of the living-room floor, I felt as if I'd fallen into a nightmare." She was crying once again, but this time they were silent tears that slipped down her cheeks. These tears touched Johnna more deeply than her earlier sobs had done.

"Erin." Johnna stood and touched Erin's shoulder gently. "You don't have to do this."

Erin stepped away from her as if she found Johnna's touch painful. "But I do." She drew a deep breath. "I would have gladly taken a beating from Richard every day of my life if it would have saved my mother's life." Her tearful eyes held a bleakness that pierced through Johnna. "Despite her faults and weaknesses, she was all I had."

She began to pace in front of Johnna and once again tears seeped from her eyes. "It wasn't until they had taken her body away and the sheriff and all his men had left that it hit me. I knew if I didn't hang on to something or someone, I'd lose my mind."

She placed her hands on either side of her head, as if she still feared her mind would slip from her grasp. "Seeing my mom that way, all the blood, knowing that somebody had come into our place and done that to her...that it could have happened when I'd been home and I could have been murdered, too... All that whirled around and around in my mind until I thought I'd go mad."

"And so you reached out for Jerrod," Johnna said softly, knowing that was exactly where all this was leading.

Erin nodded. "I think we were both a little crazy that night. What we did had nothing to do with love or desire. It was about survival. It was about seeing death up close and personal and needing to affirm life. Can you understand that?"

Yes, she could understand, Johnna thought. Wasn't it those very emotions that had prompted her to take Jerrod to her bed the night before? The terror of the break-in and assault, the need to hold on to somebody, the desire to remove the horror and lose herself in mindless passion?

"Johnna, can you understand and forgive me? Forgive him?" Erin stood before her, her eyes radiating pain. "It didn't mean anything to either of us. He loved you so very much. You were his entire world, his everything."

Johnna embraced Erin, unable to sustain any anger for the woman who had suffered so much and for a single moment had sought solace in the arms of the man Johnna had loved.

Her emotions where Jerrod was concerned were more complicated, and she didn't even try to work through them at the moment.

Erin finally stepped out of Johnna's embrace. "I swear to you, Johnna, by everything I hold dear, I did not kill Richard. Yes, I was having an affair and I know that looks bad now, but it had nothing to do with Richard's murder."

Johnna nodded, a renewed burst of grief sweeping through her. *He loved you so very much.* Erin's words rang in her head, in her heart. Had Jerrod truly loved her? Had she been his everything? Or had theirs been a youthful passion that would have never sustained itself with time and maturity?

She would never know, for that moment in time was gone, swept away by tragic circumstances and youthful mistakes. Nor could that moment in time ever be reclaimed. Too many years had passed, too many tears had been shed.

Besides, she'd always known the happiness she shared with Jerrod wouldn't last forever. She'd spent the entire time she'd been with him waiting for the other shoe to drop, knowing from experience that nothing good ever lasts.

"Can we keep Dale out of this?" Erin asked, pulling Johnna from her thoughts.

Johnna frowned. "I can't make any promises, Erin. I want to talk to him, check out his alibi for the night of Richard's murder. But if Chet Maxwell gets wind of your affair, I can promise you he'll beat it to death as a motive for you to get rid of Richard."

She didn't tell Erin that dragging Dale into it might be the only way to cast reasonable doubt to the jury. "And now I've got to run. I have to be in court later this afternoon and I've got a million things to do. I'll be in touch."

She said goodbye, then joined Harriet and Jerrod in the dining room, where they were chatting with Rose Sanders, the pretty owner of the establishment.

"Hi, Rose," Johnna said.

"Hey, Johnna." Rose offered her a sweet smile. "Want some coffee?"

"No thanks. I need to get going." She looked at Jerrod, who stood and finished his coffee. "Harriet, I'll call you," she said over her shoulder as they left.

Minutes later Johnna and Jerrod were again in her car, heading back to their respective houses. Johnna's thoughts were still reeling with the information that it had been on the night of Erin's mother's murder that Jerrod and Erin had slept together.

She found she *wanted* the anger that had sustained her through the years, but no matter how deeply she dug into her heart, she could find not a vestige of that emotion.

Instead, she was thinking about how dreadful the night must have been for Jerrod. He'd seen the lifeless body of Tabitha Warren, had smelled her spilled blood.

He'd been the only one there when Erin had fallen to pieces, when the horror and loss had been at its peak. And he'd been nothing more than a kid himself.

"Penny for your thoughts," he said, breaking the silence between them.

"At the moment it's impossible to pick any thought in particular to sell to you," she replied, then shot him a quick smile. "Besides, my thoughts are worth far more than a mere penny."

He returned her smile. "Johnna, about last night..." he began.

"Please, Jerrod. I can't talk about that now." It was true. Her head was too filled with confusion about the night they'd shared, about her feelings for him and what she'd just learned. "Right now the most important thing I can do is stay focused on the upcoming trial. Erin has to be my top priority.''

He paused a moment, as if he'd like to argue. ''Did she tell you anything else that might help in her defense?'' he asked finally.

She was grateful he was abiding by her wishes that they not discuss the night before. ''No, but she also didn't tell me anything more that might hurt her defense.''

''What's this about cash deposits being made into Richard's account?''

Johnna explained to him what Judd had told her. ''And you think it's possible it's blackmail money?'' he asked.

''Truthfully, I don't know what to think,'' she replied. ''But if it is blackmail money, I keep wondering who Richard might have been blackmailing and about what? And then I keep thinking about those news clippings he had hidden in his closet.''

''You think Richard knew something about Erin's mother's murderer?'' Jerrod asked as she pulled into her driveway.

She turned off the ignition and turned to face him, trying desperately to stay focused on their conversation and not what Erin had told her. ''I don't know what to think,'' she said again, unsure if she was talking about Richard Kramer or about Jerrod. ''I need to read the clippings Richard had and the files on the Warren murder again. Maybe I missed something the first time around.''

''Want another pair of eyes?'' he asked.

"Okay," she agreed after a moment of hesitation. She needed time to sort things out where he was concerned, but at the moment untangling the tragedies of Erin Kramer's life seemed far easier than figuring out what she wanted, if anything, from Jerrod McCain.

Jerrod followed her to her front door, wondering what it had been that Erin had shared with her that had made such a profound difference in her mood.

She'd been angry when they'd driven to the bed-and-breakfast, as angry as he'd ever seen her. Even while she'd been questioning Erin, anger had still radiated from her, evident in the sharp tone of her voice and the short steps she'd taken while pacing the room.

But something had happened when Erin had spoken to Johnna alone. Something that had driven away the anger and left in its wake a quiet, introspective mood.

He'd wanted to talk about last night. He'd wanted to tell her that making love to her again after all these years had been amazing, that he felt that his heart was finally home.

Too soon. He knew he was pushing too fast. He had to remember that although she'd hurt him terribly the night he'd told her about sleeping with Erin, it had been a hurt responding to the hurt he'd inflicted on her.

On that night so long ago he'd never gotten an opportunity to explain the situation properly to her.

He'd blurted out to Johnna that he'd slept with Erin and shouldn't have been surprised that she'd called him names and ordered him out of her life then and there.

"How's your father adjusting to your move?" she asked as she unlocked her front door.

Jerrod heaved a deep sigh. "Not as well as I'd hoped," he admitted, the subject one of enormous worry and guilt. "He stays in his room, only coming out to eat meals, then returning to his room. And I haven't figured how yet, but somehow he's still getting booze from somewhere."

They stepped into Johnna's living room, where she dropped her purse and her car keys on the coffee table. "Come on back—I've got the file and the clippings in my office."

He followed her down the hallway, pausing for just a moment as they passed her bedroom. The bed was still unmade, the blankets twisted in evidence of their lovemaking the night before.

A burst of heat exploded in the pit of his stomach at the sight of that bed. Mentally, consciously, he tamped down his desire. She had not brought him here for another bout in the bedroom, much to his dismay.

He followed her into the smaller second bedroom, where the only furnishings were a desk, a chair and a bookcase. Manila folders filled the space beside the computer. She began shuffling through the folders, a frown deepening across her forehead.

"Where is it?" she muttered. She began to throw

files on the floor next to the desk, her hands moving more frantically with each passing moment.

"What's wrong?" he asked.

"The file—the Warren file. It should be here right on top, but it isn't." More files fell to the floor, scattering papers everywhere.

Jerrod walked over to stand beside her, the scent of her perfume playing havoc with his hormones. "Are you sure you put it here?"

She stopped her motions and stood perfectly still, her frown deepening. "I read over it yesterday, then when I finished, I brought it in here and set it on the desk. Yes, I'm sure it was here."

"You didn't take it into your bedroom, instead of in here?"

"No. I'm positive I put it here." She reached a hand up and touched the wound at her hairline. "It was here until last night." Her eyes held his intently. "It was here before the break-in and now it isn't."

Jerrod held her gaze as the implications of her words spun through his head. "So that guy last night broke in here and took the file? But why?"

Again she reached up and touched her forehead, as if thinking about the break-in caused her head to ache. "I don't know, but not only is the file from the case gone, the clippings I got from Richard Kramer's house are gone, as well."

"You need to call Sheriff Broder," he said, stating the obvious. "I just don't get it. What could anyone hope to gain by stealing those files?"

"I'm making somebody nervous," she said, her

eyes gleaming unnaturally bright. "Erin's mother's murder and Richard Kramer's murder are somehow tied together. I know it. I feel it in my gut."

"I don't like this, Johnna. I don't like it at all." He moved around the desk to stand directly in front of her. Reaching a hand up, he gently touched the place where she'd been hit the night before.

"Nervous people sometimes strike out at those making them nervous." He trailed his fingertips down her forehead to the smooth skin of her cheek. "A couple of inches' difference and you might have been blinded...or worse."

He felt rather than heard her tiny gasp of breath as his fingers smoothed over her soft lips. But it wasn't desire that raced through his veins, it was fear—fear for her safety.

He knew it was useless to tell her to back off, to stop digging into the Warren and Kramer cases. He could beg, plead and demand, but he knew she would do what she felt was right no matter what the possible consequences. And that was part of what he loved about her.

"You have to promise me you'll be careful," he said softly, his fingers lingering on her mouth. "I'm worried about you."

She stepped away from his touch. "I can take care of myself." She walked around the desk and headed out of the room. "I need to call the sheriff."

Jerrod followed just behind and sat on the sofa as she picked up the phone and dialed the appropriate number. *He loved her.* The emotion flooded him with warmth.

He'd loved her as a young man and he loved her now. The intervening years didn't matter. Nothing had changed in his heart, and he had a feeling that no matter what happened between them, he'd go to his grave loving her.

Last night, as he'd held her in his arms, he hadn't just made love to her, he'd made a commitment to her in his soul. Now all he had to do was hope and pray that eventually she'd make the same kind of commitment to him.

Chapter 10

Dusk had just begun to fall as Johnna pulled up in front of the old trailer where Erin had once lived with her mother. Even the lush golden hues of twilight couldn't soften the pervasive ugliness of the small, nearly abandoned trailer park.

She wasn't sure why she'd come here. She and Jerrod had met with Sheriff Broder and reported the missing files, then Johnna had left to go to her office and pick up what she needed for the client she'd represented in court that afternoon.

When court had concluded for the day, she'd gone back to her office. After finishing up some paperwork and giving instructions to her secretary, she'd then headed out, intending to go to the ranch and put in a few hours.

Instead of ending up at the ranch, however, she'd

come here. To think for a few minutes. Discovering that the files had been stolen had not only shocked her, but positively electrified her.

If she'd had any doubts about Erin's innocence in Richard's murder, they had banished the minute she'd realized the files had been stolen.

She shrugged out of her suit jacket and tossed it into the back seat, then stepped out of the car and into the heat of early evening.

Not looking for anything in particular, she walked around the perimeter of Tabitha Warren's trailer. She knew that Erin had continued to live here after her mother's death until the time she'd married Richard.

How horrible it must have been to live your youth in such a dismal place, then to have to continue living here with the stains of your mother's blood on the floor, the memory of her murder in your head.

Had Richard discovered something about Tabitha's murder? Had he been blackmailing the killer and finally the killer had grown tired of paying the price?

She frowned and kicked at an old, rusty beer can. She could make a great case based on speculation and conjecture, but what she needed were cold, hard facts, and they seemed to be in short supply.

As she returned to the front of the trailer, her gaze swept across the narrow, graveled lane to the place where Jerrod had spent his miserable childhood.

She thought of the relationship between Erin and Jerrod, two people who had grown up a mere stone's throw from one another. They had been two people whose friendship had been cemented by a common background and the contempt of a town who found their very presence an embarrassment.

She slid back into her car and started the engine, wanting a blast of the air conditioner to cool her off. She leaned her head back against the seat and closed her eyes, her mind filling with thoughts of Jerrod.

Even all those years ago she'd known that he'd had a special friendship with Erin. He'd often shared with Johnna pieces of that friendship, telling her what he and Erin had talked about that day. She'd known that Jerrod looked out for Erin, was like the big brother Erin hadn't had.

Johnna had felt no real jealousy because she'd been so certain she and nobody else owned Jerrod's heart. He was Erin's friend, but he was Johnna's lover, her life.

And then had come the night after Tabitha Warren's murder when she'd met Jerrod as always at their usual spot, at the end of the lane that led from the Delaney ranch to the outer road. They always met there, then hand in hand they would walk down the road to a small grove of trees that had become their special place—the place where they talked and dreamed and made love.

But this night was different. She'd heard a rumor in town that day, a horrible rumor that Jerrod and Erin had been together the night before—not as friends, but as lovers. It had been a friend of Erin's who had repeated the rumor to her.

Johnna had angrily pronounced the girl a liar, then had spent the rest of the day with a cold chill wrapped around her heart as she waited for night and her rendezvous with Jerrod.

He'd met her at the right time and the right place, but she knew immediately by the darkness in his eyes that something was dreadfully wrong.

"Johnna," he'd said, his hands grasping her by the shoulders, "I have to tell you something… Something happened… Erin and I…we…"

That was all he'd had an opportunity to say. Instantly she'd known. He didn't have to say the words. She'd known in her heart, where the pain pierced her so sharply she'd felt as if death was imminent.

She'd wrenched away from his grasp. "You slept with her."

She'd waited only a moment for a protest of innocence, a statement to the contrary, but all she'd gotten from him was a guilty, haunted expression. The pain had subsided as rage took over, a rage she embraced to keep that pain at bay.

With the coolness of the air conditioner blowing on her, she reached up to place her hands on her cheeks and was surprised to realize she was weeping.

No deep, wrenching sobs racked her, rather, the tears oozed from her as if squeezed from the depths of her. She realized now that the haunted glaze in Jerrod's eyes probably hadn't been guilt, but rather horror. The horror of a young man who had seen death, a violent, brutal death, up close.

Johnna had given him no opportunity to explain anything to her. She couldn't even remember exactly what she'd said to him at the time, but she'd screamed and yelled and ordered him out of her sight, out of her life.

He'd turned and disappeared into the night. And for the next nine years she hadn't seen or heard from him.

How different would their lives have been had she given him an opportunity to explain that night? Would it have made any difference? Would the hurt have not been so all-consuming?

She swiped her cheeks with the back of her hand, then put the car into gear and pulled out of the trailer park. Driving the deserted two-lane highway toward the family ranch, she wondered if fate was giving Jerrod and her a second chance.

But even if she was offered a second chance, would she take it? She'd learned from her father to guard against her emotions, to never allow herself to be vulnerable to anything or anyone. For a brief space in time, she'd let down her guard and allowed Jerrod into places she'd never before allowed anyone.

She wasn't sure if she was capable of letting down her guard again. She had grown so accustomed to being alone, to keeping up barriers that allowed nobody into her heart, she didn't know if she knew how to be any different.

And then there was her little secret. A little secret named Miranda.

Webs of grief wrapped around her heart as she thought of her and Jerrod's baby. Their daughter.

If she continued to see Jerrod, if she had any hope of a relationship with him, eventually she would have to tell him about Miranda.

How would he take the news that she had gotten pregnant with his child and hadn't contacted him to tell him the news? She could plead the case that she hadn't known where he'd gone after he'd left Inferno, and certainly that was true.

But it wasn't as if she hadn't had the resources to find him. He would have remained in touch with his uncle, and she could have gotten his address from Cyrus. So why hadn't she?

Because she'd been too angry, because she hadn't wanted to share anything more with Jerrod McCain. She'd consciously willed herself to expel him from her heart and from her mind.

She turned through the gates that led to the Delaney Dude Ranch. She'd always believed she would never forgive Jerrod for his betrayal, but she'd been wrong. She had forgiven him. The problem was, once he heard about Miranda and how she was responsible for Miranda's death, he would never, ever forgive her.

Parking the car, she shoved thoughts of Miranda and Jerrod out of her head. She couldn't think about that now. She needed to focus on working at the ranch and Erin's court case. She couldn't afford to be distracted.

The moment she stepped out of her car, she knew that April, Mark's wife and the ranch's social director, had arranged a barbecue for the guests. The scent of grilling meat rode the air, along with the chatter of people milling around beneath a large, colorful canopy in the yard.

Luke stood before the grill, flipping burgers and turning hot dogs, basting ribs and flirting with the female guests. Remembering how sharp she'd been with him that morning, she walked over to where he was working.

"Hi," she said. "Sorry about this morning."

"There's nothing to be sorry for," he replied. "You were right. I do drink too much. And I don't get enough sleep and I don't eat right." He flashed her the smile that made female hearts palpitate all over the county. "But I'm having fun."

"Luke, when are you going to stop playing at life and start living it?" she asked.

He slapped a hot dog into a bun and handed it to her. "I guess that will happen when I stop having fun." Their conversation drew to a halt as several guests wandered over for food.

Johnna headed for the office in the main house, steeling herself for an encounter with Matthew. He was in the inner office, seated at the desk where he took care of all the paperwork running a business involved.

"Hi, Matthew," she said.

He looked up, lines of tension striped across his forehead. She couldn't remember a time when those lines hadn't been there.

"I was wondering if you were going to come in this evening," he said as he stood and walked toward her.

"Why wouldn't I come in this evening?"

"I heard you had a little excitement at your place last night—a break-in? Why didn't you call us?"

The level of his voice rose, and as usual Johnna felt as if he was yelling at her. "I had to hear about a break-in at my sister's house from Sam Clegg."

"Sam Clegg? What was he doing out here?" she asked, trying to ignore the feeling of ineptitude that always rose inside her when she spoke with Matthew. It was like standing before her stern, forbidding father.

"We had a little theft problem this morning with one of the guests. She was certain somebody had made off with her wedding rings. She insisted she'd placed them on the sink in the bathroom last night and this morning they were gone."

"Were they stolen?"

Matthew shook his head. "Sam found them on the floor by the nightstand next to her bed, which jogged her memory that she hadn't put them in the bathroom, after all."

He sighed heavily and raked a hand through his thick, dark hair. "Just one of many irritations of running a dude ranch." His blue gaze drifted up to the wound at her hairline. "So what's the deal about this break-in? What did you do? Make somebody mad with that sharp tongue of yours?''

Usually the way she dealt with Matthew was much the way she'd always dealt with her father—with defensive rebellion and hardheadedness.

She bit back the sarcastic reply that automatically leaped to her lips. ''I guess the man who broke into my place last night got mad when I woke up in the middle of him stealing some of my files. He decided to give me a crack over the head—but don't worry, I'm fine.''

''Does this have to do with the Kramer case?'' He didn't wait for her reply. ''I told you not to get tangled in that.'' He opened his mouth to continue a rant, but Johnna stopped him by reaching up and planting a kiss on his cheek.

He stepped back from her, his face registering the kind of shock he might have exhibited if she'd deliberately poked a finger in his eye. ''Why did you do that?'' he asked softly.

''Because you worry too much. You work too hard, and why should I have to explain giving my brother a kiss on the cheek?''

''Because you've never done it before.''

She studied him for a long moment. ''And there's something sad about that, isn't there?'' She spun on her heel, feeling as if she needed some air. ''I'm going to go find April and see if there's anything I can help with. I'll be back later.''

He didn't say anything as she left the room. She hadn't really expected him to. Was it possible to heal many years of a dysfunctional family relationship with conversation?

Each of the Delaney heirs had coped with their father's abuse in their own way, and Johnna had a feeling that even though their father was gone, they were still coping with the residual effects.

She had to admit, part of her problem with Matthew was that she'd always known he had what she'd desperately yearned for—the love of their father. Of all the children, Matthew had been Adam's favorite. He'd been the least likely to catch a backhand or vicious condemnation.

As she stepped out into the fading light of day, she tried not to think about the family relationship. At the moment it seemed every bit as tangled in her mind as Richard Kramer's murder, every bit as confusing as her feelings for Jerrod.

For the next several hours she helped the ranch hands clean up after the barbecue. By the time night had blanketed the ranch, she went back into the office and worked another couple of hours on the new brochure Matthew wanted to get out in the fall.

It was after eleven when she finally decided to call it a day and head back home. She stepped outside, the warmth of the night wrapping around her. Instantly she thought of Jerrod's arm wrapping around her, holding her tightly and keeping her warm.

She knew Jerrod wanted to try again, wanted to renew their relationship and see if this time they couldn't get it right; she'd have to be dumber than dirt not to realize it. His desire to resume a relationship with her was there in the haunting blue depths of his eyes, in each word that he spoke to her.

You don't have to tell him, a little voice whispered in her head as she got into her car. You don't have to tell him about Miranda. Only her brothers knew about the child she'd lost, and because she'd been living in Phoenix, they had no idea who the father had been or exactly when it had happened.

Could she build her relationship with him based on a lie? A lie of omission, certainly, but a lie nevertheless.

"No." The word came out of her mouth as she started her car. No, if she was going to build anything with Jerrod, it had to be built on truth. She had to tell him about the baby he'd lost, the little dark-haired girl he'd never gotten to hold...to love.

As she pulled out of the ranch lane and onto the deserted highway, she flicked on her high beams to help pierce the deep darkness of the night.

Suddenly her head snapped back, then forward to the accompaniment of a loud crashing noise. Her foot slipped off the gas and her gaze shot to the rearview mirror as she realized she'd been hit from behind.

Her heart lurched with a sickening thud. She'd looked both ways before pulling out onto the highway, but apparently the car or whatever it was had been in a blind spot.

She braked to a stop and opened her door, intending to get out and making sure the person who'd hit her was all right, but she didn't get the opportunity. Once again her car was smashed from behind, the motion slamming her door shut and forcing a cry from her lips.

The sound of a racing engine shot horror through her as she looked in her rearview mirror, saw the shape of some sort of vehicle and realized it was preparing to hit her again.

She jammed her foot down on the gas pedal, peeling rubber against the blacktop in an effort to escape. She heard the sharp squeal of tires as the vehicle behind her also exploded forward.

A truck, she thought with another glance in her rearview mirror. Although it didn't have any lights on, she thought it might be a pickup.

For the first time in her life she desperately wished she had a race car, instead of the reliable four-cylinder compact that got great gas mileage.

Once again she was rammed from behind. The steering wheel was wrenched from her hands by the force. She screamed.

In her bouncing headlights she saw the grove of trees that had been the place for her and Jerrod's long-ago secret trysts. Trees—too close. Her car was out of control.

Too late, she pressed hard on the brake, fighting to control the careering car, but even as she braked, she felt the truck behind her make contact with her bumper and push her.

Faster, faster, it shoved her forward as if her car was a bullet and it was a gun.

The trees rose before her, giant pillars in the stark beam of her lights. She only had time to scream again and raise her hands in front of her face.

Jerrod ran down the hallway of the small Inferno hospital toward the emergency room, his heart thundering as loudly as his footsteps on the tiled floor.

It had been around eleven that the first tendril of anxiety had taken up residency in the pit of his stomach. He'd been sitting on his half-finished front porch since dusk and knew that Johnna wasn't home. He'd remembered her mentioning that morning she was going out to the Delaney ranch to put in a few hours of work.

But by eleven, he'd started to get worried. In the days since he'd moved in across the street from her, he'd come to know her usual routine.

She started early in the mornings. He often saw her kitchen light on when dawn had not yet broken. But she was always home by eleven.

By eleven-thirty the tendril of anxiety had grown and by midnight it had transformed from uneasiness to panic.

At midnight he'd checked on his father, who was snoring loudly, then had jumped in his car and taken off to look for her. He'd driven by her office downtown, then by the bed-and-breakfast to see if she might have had a late-night meeting with Erin or Harriet. Her car wasn't at either place.

He'd taken off toward the ranch. Just before he'd

reached the ranch lane, he'd seen her car—and his heart had momentarily stopped beating.

The small red car was nosed into a tree, the front of the car crumbled like a ball of aluminum foil and the windshield shattered.

A black pickup truck sat nearby, the front end damaged.

A wrecker from one of the town's gas stations was in the process of hooking up the car to tow it away. As Jerrod raced from his car, he spied Sheriff Broder and Deputy Clegg standing together watching the car being readied for towing.

"Where is she?" Jerrod asked urgently, his heartbeat so wildly out of control he felt as if he was on the verge of a heart attack. "Where's Johnna?"

"They took her to the hospital," Broder said.

"How bad?"

"She was unconscious, Jerrod. But I think she'll be okay."

Jerrod didn't even wait for Broder to get the entire sentence out of his mouth. He turned and raced back to his car.

Now as he hurried down the hall toward the emergency room, he sent a hundred prayers to heaven. He swept past the nurse at the desk, ignoring her faint protest.

"I'm telling you, Doc, I'm fine now. I just want to go home." The voice came from behind the curtains of a nearby examining room.

Jerrod's legs nearly buckled beneath him as relief flooded him. That voice was Johnna's. And if she could talk, then she had to be all right.

"I must insist that you spend the night under observation," a male voice, apparently the doctor's, replied.

"Johnna?" Jerrod called through the curtain. He didn't want to wait. Even though he could hear her voice, knew she was all right, he needed to see her and make absolutely certain.

"Jerrod, you can come in," she answered.

He shoved the curtain aside and entered the examining room, instantly recognizing the doctor as a former classmate from Inferno High School. "Johnny Howerton," he greeted the doctor with his hand outstretched, but his gaze went directly to Johnna.

Clad in a gown, she sat on the edge of an examining table. A large bruise had begun to blossom in the center of her forehead.

"So you did make it through medical school," Jerrod said to the doctor, remembering that becoming a doctor had been his goal in high school.

"I did, and I enjoyed your sermon Sunday, although I had to leave early."

"If you two are through with the little reunion, I'd like to get out of here," Johnna said.

"I heard Dr. Howerton insist that you spend the night," Jerrod replied.

"She hit her head on the steering wheel and was knocked unconscious. Although she's shown no signs of a concussion, I'd like to keep her under observation."

"I promise you, I'm fine," Johnna said as she slid off the table to stand on the floor. "I was only out for a few minutes. You know how hardheaded we Delaneys are. All I've got now is a headache." She looked from the doctor to Jerrod. "I just want to go home."

"Johnna, I know you live alone, and I don't want you to be alone tonight," Dr. Howerton explained.

"I'll make sure she isn't left alone," Jerrod said.

"Great, then I'm out of here," Johnna declared as she reached for her clothing, which was draped across a nearby chair.

Jerrod and Dr. Howerton stepped out of the examining room, and while Johnna got dressed, the doctor explained to Jerrod what he should watch for in Johnna over the next several hours.

"She's probably going to be sore as hell," the doctor said as he handed Jerrod several samples of pain medication. "She's got some scrapes and cuts on her arms, and bruises are probably going to continue to show up." He shook his head. "She was incredibly lucky."

At that moment Johnna stepped out of the examining room and joined them. "Let's get out of here," she said to Jerrod. When she reached a hand up to touch the bruise on her forehead, he noticed that her hand was trembling.

Jerrod placed an arm around her shoulders and drew her closer to him. She didn't protest; rather, she leaned into him as if she needed his strength.

"If you feel funny in any way, call me," Dr. Howerton said.

"I promise," Johnna said.

She and Jerrod didn't speak until she was safely

buckled into the passenger seat of his car and he was behind the wheel. "Thanks for helping me get out of there. I didn't want to spend the rest of the night in the hospital."

"No problem," he replied. "So what happened?"

"Somebody driving a pickup truck tried to kill me," she said.

"It wasn't an accident?" he asked, shock rolling through him. Surely she was mistaken. She was still shaken up from the break-in the night before and maybe had mistaken an accident for something more ominous.

"No way," she said firmly. "It was quite deliberate. The truck didn't just hit me once. It kept on hitting me, then pushed me into the tree."

Jerrod started his car, his blood running cold as he contemplated her words. What can of worms had she opened? Who was responsible for all this? "Who does the truck belong to?" he asked as he pulled away from the hospital.

"Tom Mayfield. According to Broder, Tom reported it stolen about an hour before it was found with mine."

"And who found you?"

"Sam Clegg. Thank God he was out looking for Tom's truck and just happened to come upon the wreck. I came to when he opened the car door and called my name."

"So I guess the driver of the truck was long gone."

She nodded, then winced slightly. "By the time

Sam got on the scene, whoever was driving that truck had hightailed it out of there.''

She leaned her head back against the seat and sighed. "For the past two nights I've been terrified—first by an intruder in my home, then by some crazed driver in a pickup. Broder seems to think the truck was stolen by some teenager who was probably under the influence of drugs or alcohol, and that the accident was just that, an accident.''

"But we know better.''

"Damn right,'' she retorted angrily.

Jerrod was grateful to hear the anger in her voice. It told him she was feeling better, stronger.

"That truck wasn't being driven by some drunk or stoned teenager. I have irrefutable evidence to that.''

He pulled into her driveway and switched off the ignition. "What kind of irrefutable evidence?'' he asked.

She unbuckled her seat belt and reached down to pick up her purse from the floor. As he watched, she reached into the purse and pulled out a small piece of paper. As she handed it to him, he noted that she was trembling again.

He turned on the dome light and looked down at the paper. An icy chill went through him as he read the words written in bold, black marker:

LET SLEEPING DOGS LIE OR YOU ARE GOING TO DIE.

Chapter 11

Johnna leaned her head back against the cool porcelain of her bathtub as steam from the running hot water filled the room. The moment she and Jerrod had walked into her house, all she'd wanted to do was take a hot bath and try to release the tension that seemed to have tied her entire body in knots of pain.

Jerrod was in her kitchen, making her a cup of tea. She figured she'd drink a little, then shove him out the door and go to bed. She felt as if she could sleep for a month. All she had to do was get past the fear that made closing her eyes and giving in to the vulnerability of sleep seem impossible.

The horror of recent events had produced a chill in her body she couldn't seem to warm. Even the hot bath wasn't having the desired effect.

Every time she closed her eyes, she saw in her mind's eye the black shape of that truck. She still could hear the roar of the engine as the driver readied himself to attack her. The memory of that noise caused another chill to race up her spine.

She could have been killed. As far as she was concerned, what she'd survived was an attempted murder. Who was responsible?

She turned off the water, then stood and grabbed a towel to dry off. Minutes later, clad in a warm, fluffy robe and with her hair finger-combed into place, she left the bathroom and headed for the kitchen.

Jerrod was there, seated at the table, and when she appeared in the doorway, he looked at her in surprise. "You aren't dressed?"

She frowned and slid into the seat across from him where he had a cup of hot tea awaiting her. "I'm just going to bed. Why would I get dressed again?"

"You don't think you're sleeping here, do you?" He raised a dark eyebrow, his features filled with tension.

"Where else would I be sleeping?" She spooned some sugar into her tea, then took a sip.

"You can't stay here, Johnna. You can't stay all alone." He leaned forward and eyed her intently. "I'm sure Sheriff Broder expressed concern when you showed him the note that was left in your purse."

She gazed into her cup, knowing that what she

was about to confess would upset him. "I didn't tell Sheriff Broder about the note. I didn't tell anyone about it but you."

"Why?" He looked at her incredulously. "Don't you think it's important? It's certainly proof that what happened tonight wasn't just an accident."

"Of course it's important." She wrapped her hands around her cup, seeking the warmth contained within. "I was going to tell him and eventually I probably will, but I need some time to think. And the truth is…I don't know who to trust."

"Jeffrey Broder is the sheriff—surely you can trust him. He was just a boy when Erin's mother was murdered."

Johnna sighed and took another sip of her tea. "But his father was the sheriff at the time. I know it sounds crazy, Jerrod, but I really don't know what to think."

Jerrod leaned back in his chair and frowned thoughtfully. "Okay, so we don't know who we can trust."

His use of *we* instead of *you* warmed her as the bath and the tea had been unable to do. "I mean, I doubt the Broders are guilty of anything, but the bogeyman is after me and I don't know who he is."

She tensed to ward off a shiver. "What I don't understand is why he didn't just kill me. I mean, I was unconscious long enough for him to reach into my car, get my purse and tuck that note inside. He could have just as easily put a bullet in my head or wrapped his hands around my neck. Why didn't he?''

Jerrod's eyes darkened. "I don't know. Apparently whoever it is doesn't want you dead—he just wants you off the case.''

"But which case? The note said to let sleeping dogs lie. It has to be referring to Tabitha Warren's murder.''

"All I know is that you can't stay here alone. Why don't you pack a bag and let me take you to the ranch? Your brothers are there to look after you, and with all the guests you'll be highly visible.''

"No way,'' Johnna replied flatly. She would not run and hide at the ranch. Although she knew it was irrational, it felt too much like surrender, as if she was admitting weakness to her dead father.

"Johnna, it isn't safe for you here, and the doctor said you need observation.'' Jerrod stood and stared at her, his gaze as intense as she'd ever seen. "Okay, if you won't go to the ranch, then there's only one other alternative.'' Without saying another word, he turned and strode out of the kitchen.

Johnna jumped out of her chair and hurriedly followed him down the hallway. "Jerrod, what are you doing?''

"I'm taking charge,'' he replied. He went into her bedroom and crossed to the closet. Pushing back clothes, he located an overnight bag and pulled it out, then opened it on the bed. "Pack,'' he commanded.

"Jerrod, I am not going to the ranch.'' She sank

onto the bed next to the suitcase. "My head is pounding and I'm too exhausted to fight with you. But there's no way I'm going to run to the ranch with my tail tucked between my legs."

"Then don't fight with me. Throw some things in the suitcase. I'm not taking you to the ranch."

"Then where?" she asked.

"Across the street. To my place."

Johnna looked at him in surprise. He walked over and took her hands in his, his blue eyes intense. "Johnna, I couldn't sleep at night knowing you were over here all alone. You've had two threats on your life, and I'm not willing to believe you have the nine lives of a cat."

His hands squeezed hers. "You were lucky you weren't hurt more badly or even killed in the accident tonight. I've got a spare room and I want you to stay there until Erin's trial is over."

"But what would people think? You're a minister, Jerrod," she protested, although she had to admit the idea held appeal.

If she looked in her heart, she knew she'd find fear, and she really didn't want to stay here in her house all alone. The taste of her fear lingered in her mouth and in the chill that had taken up residency in her entire body.

Jerrod shot her a wry grin. "Since when do I care what people think? Besides, nobody should say too much—after all, my father lives there, too." He pulled her off the bed. "Come on, throw a few things in a bag and let's get going. It's late and you need some sleep.''

This time she didn't protest. It took her only minutes to gather what she needed for the night and the next day.

Jerrod left the bedroom to rinse the teacups in the kitchen, and while he was gone, she changed from the robe to a pair of jeans and a T-shirt, then grabbed the overnight case and met him at the front door.

''Thank you, Johnna,'' he said as they left her house.

''Thank you for what?''

''For not arguing with me about staying at my place. I'd hate to have to spend the next couple of weeks camped out in your yard to make sure nobody tried to hurt you.''

''You'd do that for me?''

He reached out and touched her cheek softly. ''In a heartbeat.''

She stepped back from him, disturbed by how easily he could shoot an electric thrill through her with the simplest of touches. ''Why don't you drive your car across the street and I'll walk.''

He hesitated and she handed him her suitcase. ''I can manage to walk across the street without anything happening. Besides, I'm starting to feel like I've been beaten up. I don't want to have to crawl in and out of a car another time this evening.''

''Okay.'' He threw the suitcase into the back seat, got behind the wheel and before Johnna had taken a single step, started the engine.

As he pulled out of her driveway and into his own, Johnna rubbed a hand lightly across her forehead, where her brain seemed to be throwing itself against her skull. The headache was fierce enough to make any deep thought impossible.

She would stay at Jerrod's for tonight, but she didn't intend to stay there more than a night. She hated to impose and didn't think the close quarters would be good for either of them.

Slowly, aware of all her aches and pains, she started out across the street. By the time she reached his front door he was waiting for her, her suitcase in hand.

He opened the door, flipped on a light and gestured her inside. She looked around curiously, intrigued to see what kind of home Jerrod had made for himself.

The living room was quite masculine, but attractive, with two recliner chairs and an overstuffed sofa in matching dark-blue-patterned material. There were no knickknacks, no clutter, and the whole room smelled of lemon wax.

"Nice," she said softly.

"It's coming along," he replied. "Unfortunately the bedrooms are still rough."

"If mine has a bed, it's perfect," she replied. She drew a deep breath of exhaustion, then touched her head once again.

"Hurt?" he asked, his gaze soft, sympathetic.

"Yeah. My head hurts, my arms hurt, my legs

hurt…'' She allowed her voice to drift off. "I'm just one big aching mass of muscle.''

"Then let's get you into bed.'' He gestured to the staircase that led to the second floor. He went with her up the stairs, a hand at the small of her back.

"First door on the left,'' he said when they reached the landing.

She turned into the room and flipped on the light. He hadn't been kidding. There was a double bed and nothing else in the room. But the bed looked wonderfully enticing, with clean white sheets and two thick pillows.

"Why don't you go ahead and get into bed, then I'll bring you a couple of pain pills Dr. Howerton gave me for you,'' he suggested.

She nodded, and as he left the room she opened her suitcase, pulled out her nightshirt, then changed and crawled beneath the sheets.

The mattress welcomed her and the pillow cradled her head with downy softness. She closed her eyes for a moment, allowing her body to relax, willing her head to stop its incessant banging.

She would be safe here, and the thought eased the pounding of her head. She could sleep and not be afraid, close her eyes and not worry about bogeymen in the night.

She opened her eyes when Jerrod knocked lightly, then entered. He crossed to the bed, a glass of water in one hand and two little white pills in the other.

Sitting up, she took the pills and chased them with a sip of the water, then lay back. "I don't have an alarm clock," she said. "Would you make sure I'm up by eight? I've got a nine-o'clock meeting scheduled with Erin and Harriet."

"I'll take care of it," he said, then leaned down and pressed his lips to her cheek. The kiss was feather soft and sent a wave of warmth through her.

"Sleep well, Johnna," he murmured as she closed her eyes. "I'm in the bedroom directly across the hall if you need anything."

She didn't open her eyes or say anything. She was afraid that if she looked at him, saw the caring and concern that were in his eyes, she'd want him next to her in the bed.

She was afraid that if he pressed his lips to her cheek one more time, she'd turn her head and capture his mouth with hers. It would be so easy to fall into his arms and be warmed, be comforted.

It would be so easy to love Jerrod with the same intensity, the same sweet wonder she'd felt with him long ago. But she'd be a fool to fall into the magical possibility of any sort of a future with him.

She realized that at some point in time she'd forgiven him for his betrayal long ago. Unfortunately she had a feeling that when he found out about Miranda he would never be able to forgive her.

It was just before noon when Jerrod heard Johnna flying down the stairs. He looked up from the bacon he was frying as she entered the kitchen, her eyes wide with panic.

"Why didn't you wake me up?" she demanded

irritably. ''I asked you to. You knew I had a meeting scheduled for nine this morning.''

''Relax, Johnna. I called Erin and Harriet first thing this morning and explained everything. They're meeting you here at two. Help yourself to the coffee. Breakfast will be ready in about fifteen minutes.''

She looked as if she was about to protest his high-handedness in taking control of her schedule, but instead, the tension seeped out of her and she moved to the coffeepot.

''How did you sleep?'' he asked as she poured herself a cup, then crossed to the kitchen table to sit.

''Great. I don't think I moved all night long.'' She took a sip of coffee.

''And how do you feel?'' He smiled sympathetically. ''Your forehead is an interesting shade of purple.''

''Yeah, I noticed that. I'm sore, but not as sore as I thought I'd be.''

''Good.'' His gaze lingered on her. She looked right sitting at his table in his kitchen. Just as it had felt right knowing she was sleeping beneath his roof. The only thing that would have felt more right was her being in his bed, in his arms.

''Where's your father?''

Jerrod moved the skillet off the hot burner, then grabbed his cup of coffee and joined her at the table. ''Upstairs in his room, where he spends all his time. I thought the move would help, you know, get him away from all the memories the trailer held. But I guess the memories are in his head. When my mother left us, she didn't just break his heart, she broke his spirit.''

''Maybe you're expecting positive results too quickly,'' she suggested.

''Maybe,'' he agreed without any real hope. What was interesting to Jerrod was he'd begun to realize—and worry—that he was more like his father than he cared to admit.

Ever since the night he'd left Inferno years ago, Johnna had never been far from his thoughts, his heart. It had been thoughts of Johnna that made him work hard to make positive changes in his life. It had been the need of Johnna that had brought him back to Inferno.

Just like Jerrod's mother had forever been his father's weakness, Jerrod knew that Johnna would always be his own weakness.

Was he a fool just like his father? Hanging on to memories and destroying any chance of finding happiness with anyone else?

There were moments in the black of night that he found himself worrying that if things didn't work out between him and Johnna, if they never got their second chance at happily-ever-after, then he could wind up like his father, broken and barely alive.

At that moment the object of his thoughts walked into the kitchen. Mack McCain scowled in surprise at the sight of Johnna seated at the table.

''You didn't say nothin' about us havin' company,'' he said as he buttoned the stained shirt he'd obviously just pulled on. He walked over to pour himself a cup of coffee.

''Hi, Mr. McCain. I'm Johnna Delaney,'' Johnna said.

Jerrod's dad waved his hand in the air. ''I know who you are. My boy used to sneak off to meet you when he thought I was sleeping.''

To Jerrod's surprise Johnna's cheeks flamed red.

''That was a long time ago,'' she said.

Mack grunted. ''Guess you're old enough now that the two of you don't have to sneak around anymore.''

''Johnna's going to be staying here in the spare room for a couple of days,'' Jerrod explained. ''She's having some problems with a case she's working on, and threats have been made against her.''

Mack eased down at the table and eyed her curiously. ''Are you as hard to get along with as your daddy was?''

''Dad!'' Jerrod protested.

Johnna laughed. ''I certainly hope not.''

''He was the meanest cuss I've ever met,'' Mack said, and noisily sipped his coffee.

Jerrod opened his mouth to protest once again, but Johnna shot him a reassuring smile and lifted a hand to keep him silent.

''But then, I suppose growing up with a father like that made all of you stronger than most kids.''

Mack looked at Jerrod. ''Are we gonna eat this

morning or are we just gonna sit here at the table all day?''

Jerrod chuckled and started scrambling eggs.

As they ate breakfast, Jerrod noticed something astonishing. His father showed more animation than Jerrod had seen in him in months.

Johnna entertained, telling stories of various clients she'd represented and more than once pulling a rusty burst of laughter from Mack.

''I hope you don't mind, I'm having a meeting here with Erin McCall and an old professor friend of mine,'' Johnna said as they were finishing the meal.

''The professor, Harriet, is about your age, Dad,'' Jerrod said.

''Is that a fact,'' Mack replied, but it was obvious he'd retreated back into his shell. ''I believe I'll just go up and take a little nap,'' he said as he pushed away from the table.

Jerrod watched him leave, his heart heavy.

''Give it time, Jerrod,'' Johnna said softly, as if able to read his mind.

''I know.'' He placed a stack of dirty dishes in the sink, then turned to face her. ''It's just sometimes I wonder why I wasn't enough to pull him out of the bottle, why he couldn't love me enough to get on with life.''

''Oh, Jerrod.'' She crossed the floor, and to his surprise, wrapped her arms around his neck. Her smoke-gray eyes gazed into his. ''Don't do that. Don't make it about you. I spent too many years wondering why my father couldn't love me, wondering what I had done wrong, what I continued to do wrong.''

She placed a hand on his cheek, her fingers cool and soft. He instantly reacted to the touch and the nearness of her body. Her scent surrounded him, that faintly floral, wonderfully exotic smell that was hers alone.

''But I finally realized it wasn't about me,'' she continued. ''It was about him. And it's about your father. His weaknesses and his problems. My father being a mean son of a bitch wasn't my fault. And your father drinking too much and living in a near-stupor for most of your life isn't your fault.''

Jerrod reached up and touched her cheek, trailing his fingertips over her smooth skin. ''When did you get so smart?''

She sighed and her breasts pressed more firmly against his chest. ''I'm not so smart. If I were really smart, I'd know who killed Richard Kramer. If I were smart, I'd know who killed Tabitha Warren.''

''You're a lawyer, Johnna, not a miracle worker.''

Her wry smile sent a new wave of heat through him. ''I don't much believe in miracles. I've certainly never seen much evidence of miracles in my life.''

''I think it's a miracle that we're here together after all these years,'' he replied. ''I think it's a miracle that you're standing so close to me right now that I can smell your perfume and feel your heart beating against mine.''

Tension rippled in the air, an exciting sexual tension that sent Jerrod's blood racing through his veins. His body responded, and he saw in the depths of her eyes that she was aware of his desire.

For one suspended, golden moment in time, neither of them moved or said a word. They simply stood there holding each other, and Jerrod had never wanted her more than he did at that moment.

And in that moment he thought he saw something in her eyes, something beyond desire, something remarkably close to what he'd once seen in those beautiful gray depths.

She quickly stepped out of his embrace, as if aware of his mounting desire and eager to escape from it. "I need to get some paperwork from my house before Erin and Harriet get here. Do you want to go over there with me?"

She had closed off, shut down her emotions. He could see it in the flatness of her eyes, the rigid set of her shoulders.

"Sure," he agreed.

Timing, Jerrod reminded himself a few minutes later as he and Johnna walked across the street to her house.

The timing was all wrong for him to declare how much he still loved her, how much he wanted her to be a part of his life, a part of his future.

He only hoped that eventually the time would be right. He hoped that eventually they would have their second chance at love.

And this time he wouldn't screw it up.

Chapter 12

"Do you really think Dale Jenkins has something to do with Richard's murder?" Jerrod asked as he pulled his car into a parking space in front of the Inferno town hall.

"I doubt it," Johnna replied. "But he's the only person involved with Erin I haven't spoken to yet."

Johnna looked at her watch. Her appointment with the mayor was in ten minutes. "If there's something you need to do here in town, I'm sure I'll be fine. I doubt if anyone will make an attempt on my life in the middle of the day in the town hall."

"I don't have anything else to do. I'd like to go in with you, if you don't mind. I think it's time I introduced myself to Mayor Jenkins."

Johnna nodded and together they got out of Jerrod's car. Moments later they sat in the reception area of the mayor's office, having been told by a cool blonde that the mayor would be with them momentarily.

Jerrod sat next to her, the scent of him wrapping around her with the familiarity that both warmed her and disturbed her.

She had intended to stay with him and his father for only one night, but one night had quickly become two, then three, then four.

She told herself she was only staying because Jerrod was insistent, but the truth was, she wasn't eager to return to her home alone. There was so much comfort in sleeping and knowing Jerrod was right across the hall.

And it wasn't just at night that he played the role of bodyguard. He refused to allow her to go anywhere in town or anywhere else on her own. He even accompanied her to the ranch when she went out there to put in a few of hours of work.

She now cast him a surreptitious glance, her heart stepping up its tempo just a bit as she contemplated his handsome countenance.

In the past four days, although they were sleeping in separate bedrooms, sharing only common living space and rarely touching, she felt as if the intimacy between them had deepened beyond measure.

In the evenings, after Mack had gone to bed, she and Jerrod sat in the quiet of the living room and talked. They spoke of nothing painful, no past and no future.

They just talked of everyday things, of current events and people in town. They shared thoughts about newspaper articles, lightheartedly debated politics, and Jerrod shared his vision for a church youth group, the first meeting of which would take place that evening in his house.

Johnna knew that someday she would look back on these idyllic days spent in Jerrod's home and embrace the memory.

She couldn't remember a place or time in her life when she'd felt so contented. And that worried her.

"The Honorable Jenkins will see you now," the blonde said to them, and motioned to a door at the left of her desk.

Dale Jenkins stood at the window behind an impressive oak desk. As they entered his office, he turned and offered them a blinding smile that displayed thousands of dollars spent in dental work.

"Johnna, good to see you." He came around the desk, his hand extended.

She shook his hand curtly, then quickly introduced Jerrod.

"Ah, yes, I heard good things about your sermon last Sunday. Please, sit down." He gestured them into the two straight-backed chairs in front of his desk, then resumed his seat behind it. "It's always good to hear of locals who have left Inferno returning to the fold, so to speak," he said to Jerrod.

"There was no place else I could imagine living," Jerrod returned pleasantly, but Johnna felt Jerrod's tension and Jerrod was wondering if perhaps the slick, blond mayor was responsible for not only Kramer's death, but the break-in at her home and the ramming of her car.

"So what can I do for the two of you?" Dale looked from Johnna to Jerrod, then back again.

"We're here to discuss Erin Kramer," Johnna said.

In the depths of his brown eyes Johnna saw a flash of wariness. "Dreadful thing, the murder of Richard and all." He shook his head slowly, as if afraid to disturb the style of his hair. "You don't like to think things like that can happen in a nice town like Inferno."

"Yes, but I'm here to find out more about your relationship with Erin. When did you start sleeping with her?" Johnna asked.

It was obvious the question took him by surprise. He sat back in his chair, a slight flush creeping up his neck. For a moment Johnna thought he was going to deny everything.

He opened his mouth, sighed heavily and stared down at the top of his desk. "I guess Erin told you we were seeing each other occasionally. It was no big deal, just sort of a casual thing."

"When Erin told us about you, it didn't sound like a little casual thing," Johnna replied thinly. Erin had been so desperate to protect Dale, so sure that their love was the one good thing in her life.

Dale shrugged. "She was unhappy in her marriage. We just sort of fell into an affair. But it wasn't a big deal. We both knew the score."

"And what, exactly, was the 'score'?" Jerrod asked, his features set in granite as he stared at the man who suddenly appeared small and distasteful.

"You know—Erin was an unhappily married woman. And even though I'm single, Erin knew she wasn't the kind of woman I'll eventually choose to marry. She's a sweet kid, but she knew I wasn't ever going to marry her."

Johnna's blood simmered. What the mayor was really saying was that Erin had been trailer trash, not the right class of woman with the right kind of background to enhance his political career.

She held on to her anger and focused on the questions she wanted answered. "Did you know that Richard was beating the hell out of Erin?"

"Absolutely not!" He lifted his chin and met Johnna's gaze. "I didn't learn about that until after Richard was dead. Erin never told me. She refused to even talk about Richard when we were together."

"Where were you on the night of Richard's murder?"

Dale's features twisted into a mask of incredulous disbelief. "Surely you don't think I had anything to do with that, do you?"

"I not only need to know where you were on that particular night, but I also want to know where you were last Monday night between the hours of ten and midnight."

"This is absurd," Dale protested, and stood, as if he might intimidate her by towering above her. He frowned as if just recognizing what she'd asked. "What happened Monday night?"

"Just tell us where you were on those two nights," Jerrod said softly, his voice steel beneath smooth silk.

"The night of Richard's murder I was speaking at a meeting of the Women's League. The meeting lasted until after ten and took place at Mildred O'Neil's house. After the meeting we sat and drank coffee until just after midnight, then I went home."

"And Monday night?" Johnna asked.

Dale frowned. "Monday night I worked here until nearly eight, then I...I spent the rest of the evening with a friend." It was instantly apparent by the flush of color that once again rose from the base of his neck what kind of companion the "friend" was.

"Another unhappily married woman?" Johnna asked, not even attempting to hide her distaste.

Dale didn't reply, and in his silence was the answer.

Johnna stood, suddenly weary. "You might be the Honorable Mayor Dale Jenkins to the rest of Inferno, but there is nothing honorable about you. Come on, Jerrod, let's get out of here. I have a bad taste in my mouth."

She didn't speak again until they were back in Jerrod's car, then she exploded. "That man is the lowest of the low. I can't believe a jerk like that was elected. I swear, when he's up for reelection, I'll mount a campaign against him the likes of which he's never seen. He's pond scum. He's...he's..."

She shot a glance at Jerrod, who was grinning at her in amusement. "I can't think of anything worse than pond scum."

Jerrod's smile fell away. "But you don't think he's a murderer."

"No, I don't." Johnna sighed and rubbed her forehead, where in the past four days the bruising had finally started to fade. "He's a lowlife, an opportunist and a womanizer, but my gut says he isn't a murderer."

"So what now?" Jerrod asked as he started the car.

"I don't know," she confessed. "The trial is coming up way too fast. I need to talk to Judd, have him double-check the mayor's alibis and see if he's come up with any other information that might help us."

"How about some lunch at the diner first?"

"Lunch sounds wonderful," she said.

Within minutes they were seated at a booth in the diner and had ordered their lunch. Johnna's head was still spinning with thoughts on the case on how best to serve Erin. She did not want Erin to be a victim again.

"Let it go for a few minutes," Jerrod said softly.

She smiled ruefully, not surprised that he knew how her mind was spinning. "I can't. Time seems to be running out for Erin, and if anyone deserves a break, it's her."

Johnna picked up her knife and toyed with it. She put it down when she realized she was imagining thrusting it into Dale Jenkins's chest where his heart should have been. "I keep thinking of Erin's face when she told me about Dale, how much she wanted to protect him from any scandal. Then I see his face as he tells us his relationship with her was no big deal and I want to scream."

"Dale probably played on all Erin's vulnerabilities, all the baggage she carried from her childhood," Jerrod observed. "She didn't tell anyone she was being beaten because somewhere inside her, she believed she deserved to be beaten. And probably deep in her heart she didn't really expect anything from Dale Jenkins, because she believed she wasn't really good enough for him, anyway."

"And all of that is the baggage from where she grew up?" Johnna asked.

Jerrod smiled patiently. "I'm sure it's more than just the fact that she grew up in the trailer park. But, Johnna, there's no way you could ever understand the impact that had on our lives, how it affected not only how the townspeople viewed us, but how we saw ourselves."

"But you grew up in the trailer park, and you don't seem to have the same kind of baggage Erin has," Johnna mused.

He held her gaze. "Oh, Johnna, but I did. When I left here, I was hell-bent on proving to the world just how bad I could be. I lived up to everyone's expectations of what trailer trash was all about."

A shaft of remorse shot through Johnna, remorse so intense it momentarily took her breath away.

Memories of the night years ago unfurled in her mind. She had used words as fists, hitting him where he was most vulnerable, playing on the vulnerability of his background and the town's scorn.

"Jerrod, I'm so sorry," she whispered. She had told him she'd never expected him to be faithful because gutter trash never was.

He nodded, as if knowing instinctively exactly what she was apologizing for. "That was a night of pain for both of us. The hurt I dealt to you was no less intense than the one you dealt me back. But we were kids, Johnna, and dealing with issues and emotions we didn't have the maturity to handle."

"Yes, but I know the power of words," Johnna replied, unwilling to be easy on herself. "I grew up with my father battering me with hateful words, and I knew they could be as devastating as physical blows. I was angry, but I was also way out of line."

Jerrod leaned back in the booth, his gaze thoughtful. "Maybe in the larger scheme of things you did me a big favor."

They fell silent as the waitress arrived to serve them their meal. "Did you a favor how?" Johnna asked the moment the waitress had once again left them alone.

"If it hadn't been for that night and losing you, I would never have hit rock bottom. And without hitting rock bottom, I would never have turned my life around." He smiled at her, and in his eyes she saw his unconditional forgiveness. "And now let's talk about something else while we enjoy our meal.''

She nodded, fighting a wave of emotion she couldn't understand—a mixture of grief over what they had lost on that night so long ago and the fear that what they'd lost would never again be reclaimed.

''Have you noticed a change in my father over the past couple of days?'' Jerrod asked.

''You mean how he's suddenly making more and more appearances out of his room?'' She smiled. ''I've also noticed that whenever Harriet drops by, he appears with his hair combed and wearing a clean shirt.''

''And he isn't drinking,'' Jerrod added. ''It's not just Harriet he's responding to. It's also you and whoever joins us in the house. It's like all of a sudden he's decided to be sociable. He's looking outward, instead of wallowing in self-pity.''

She smiled wryly. ''Maybe it's one of those miracles you talk about.''

''No, I think it's all about loneliness.'' Jerrod paused to pop a French fry into his mouth, then continued, ''Dad was stuck in that trailer year after year. He didn't go anywhere and nobody came to see him. I never had friends over when I lived there. Before the move, he'd been alone most of his life, and loneliness can do terrible things to a person.''

''I could have sworn Harriet had on lipstick yesterday when she stopped by. In all the years I've known her, I've never seen her wear lipstick.''

Johnna thought of the woman who had been her mentor. "I think maybe Harriet has been lonely for a very long time, too."

"It would be nice if two kindred spirits might somehow find each other in all this mess of Erin's life," Jerrod observed.

"Yes, it would be nice if something good comes out of all this," she agreed.

His gaze held hers intently. "Trust me, Johnna, I intend to see that something good comes out of all this."

What she saw in his eyes was a warm promise, a promise she desperately wanted to believe in. She broke eye contact, knowing it would be far too easy to fall into the depths of his eyes and believe the promise that shone there. She knew he wanted to say more. Hungry desire radiated from him, but more than that was a sweet, tender yearning.

She didn't want him to say anything more. She wasn't ready to tell him about Miranda, wasn't ready to see those wonderful emotions of his transform into something ugly and unforgiving.

Not yet. Dear God, not yet.

"All I know is that I need to pull a miracle out of my hat to save Erin," she said, bringing the conversation back full circle.

"Don't discount the possibility. Miracles happen every day of the week."

"Then pray for one, Jerrod. Because we need one desperately." She frowned and focused on her food, unsure if she was talking about Erin's case or her personal relationship with Jerrod.

They finished lunch, then returned to Jerrod's house, where Johnna closed herself in her bedroom to work on her opening statement for Erin's trial.

She stretched out on the bed, a legal pad before her and a sharpened pencil in hand. She and Harriet had agreed that they were not going to depict Erin as a battered wife. However, they knew the jury would have to be told about the fight that took place between Richard and Erin on the night of the murder.

They just didn't intend to bring up past incidents of abuse. Both Harriet and Johnna were afraid that the jury would believe Erin finally killed the man who had tormented her throughout their marriage.

While the battering would have been a mitigating circumstance had Erin been guilty, their defense of her was strictly a "not guilty" strategy.

Johnna had desperately hoped she would have a suspect or several suspects to point a finger at, but no potential alternative murderer had come to light.

Nor could she tie the murder of Richard and Tabitha together and explain to the jury about the threatening notes, the break-in and her car being rammed. It would only serve to muddy the waters.

Erin was their best witness, but Johnna knew it was always dicey putting the accused on the stand. Still, they had no other alternative but to allow Erin to tell the jury what had happened that night.

Johnna must have fallen asleep, for when she

awoke and looked at her wristwatch she saw it was almost 6 p.m. She put her notes in her briefcase, straightened the bed, then opened her bedroom door.

Immediately she heard the sound of voices drifting up from the kitchen and remembered that tonight was the first meeting of the youth group. Jerrod had invited a bunch of kids for sandwiches, chips, sodas and a sermon.

She sat at the top of the stairs, listening to the sound of laughter, the deep rumble of Jerrod's voice among the obviously younger male and female voices.

She hoped this meeting went well. From the conversations she and Jerrod had shared in the past four days, she knew that reaching the youth of the town was an important part of his mission.

Thinking of their conversation over lunch, her heart ached for the boy he had been, growing up in a section of town that instantly tainted him as no good, as trash.

He'd been an angry young man, but it had been that anger, that edge, that had drawn her to him. Now that edge was gone, replaced by an inner peace she found more provocative, more magnetic than any bad-boy vibrations he'd emanated years before.

"Guess we got a houseful of young'uns."

Johnna jumped up to see Mack standing on the landing behind her. "Sounds like it." She noticed he was dressed neatly and his gray hair was combed. She even thought she smelled a faint whiff of aftershave.

"That lawyer friend of yours called earlier this afternoon while you and Jerrod were out. She said it was nothing important, that she'll talk to you in the morning." The color of his cheeks deepened slightly. "She's a headstrong woman, isn't she?"

Johnna bit back a smile. "I'd say Harriet borders on being downright stubborn."

Mack nodded. "She's got it into her head that she and I ought to go to breakfast together at the diner in the morning. I suppose it's easier to just go with her than to fight her."

"Definitely," Johnna agreed with forced soberness.

"Guess I'd better get down there and help my boy with all them kids." Mack stepped past her, then looked back. "You coming down?"

"I'll be down in just a minute or two," she replied.

"Better hurry if you want to eat. You know teenagers can put away a lot of food in a short period of time." With those words, Mack went down the stairs and disappeared into the kitchen.

Johnna once again sat on the stairs, a smile curving her lips as she thought of Mack and Harriet. Maybe Harriet was just what Mack needed—a strong woman who would pull him out of his cocoon.

Her smile faded as she heard Jerrod say something, then the appreciative laughter from his audience. He liked kids. He would have made a wonderful father.

Pain seared through her. He'd said that he wanted a family, children to nurture and to love. So what would he think of her when he discovered she'd not only lost his child, but had, in a moment of weakness, wished the baby away? And for the first and only time in her life, her wish had come true.

Chapter 13

Jerrod was riding higher than a kite, soaring with the residual excitement of the youth meeting the night before and the fact that his father had just left to have breakfast with Harriet.

For the first time in his life, he felt as if all the pieces were finally falling in line. He sat at the kitchen table and sipped his coffee, contemplating the positive changes that seemed to be happening faster than he could assimilate them.

The most amazing had been the transformation in his father. Mack McCain had been reborn. He'd put down the bottle and picked up a new sense of pride. Jerrod knew it wasn't just the presence of Harriet, but rather a combination of things.

Moving Mack out of the trailer had been the first

step. Bringing people into this house and filling it with conversation and laughter had also helped.

Mack was healing from the wounds life had dealt him, and it was a wondrous thing to see. It was as if he'd finally recognized it was time to stop looking backward and begin visualizing the future.

And that was what Jerrod had been doing, visualizing a future—a future with Johnna. He took another sip of his coffee, visions of her flittering through his head.

She confused him. One minute he felt her pulling him closer, allowing him total access to her heart, and the next moment she was shoving him away, closing off from him and leaving him cold and lonely.

Was she still punishing him for his betrayal with Erin? He'd thought, hoped, they had managed to move past that. Although they had only discussed that evening in general terms, he'd believed that she now understood why he had done what he did. He'd believed that she'd forgiven him. But had she?

The past five days with her in his home, under his roof had been a form of exquisite torture for him. He lay in his lonely bed each night and thought he could hear the sound of her breathing from the bedroom across the hall. He thought he could smell the sweet scent of her drifting into his room.

Desire had been his bedmate. It was a white, hot desire that throbbed inside him, and on more than one night he'd fought the need to creep across the hall and take her in his arms, make love to her until the sun peeked up to proclaim a new day.

Even in the evenings, when they sat and talked, desire for her thrummed inside him. He didn't want her for mere minutes, he didn't want her for the space of one dark night. He wanted her forever and always as his soul mate, his lover...his wife.

But was she ready for him to tell her the depth of his love for her? Could she relinquish the past in order to embrace a future with him?

He wanted that. Dear God, how he wanted that. He wanted her not just to be staying at his house, but to live here, make it their home. He wanted to look out from his pulpit every Sunday and see her sitting in the front row, her love for him radiating from her eyes.

At that moment the object of his thoughts, the woman of his heart, walked into the kitchen. "Good morning," he said, noting that her hair was still damp from her shower and the scent of minty soap battled with the more subtle floral fragrance of her perfume.

"Morning," she replied, and headed for the coffeemaker and the cup on the countertop that awaited her.

"Did you sleep well?" he asked as she joined him at the table.

"Like a log. What about you?" She cast him one of her full smiles that sent sweet heat rushing through him. "You were pretty wound up after your youth meeting last night."

"I'm still a little wired from it," he confessed. "It went far better than I anticipated. The kids were so open to everything."

"That's because you were good with them. You didn't condescend or preach. You just talked with them, not at them." She took a sip of her coffee. "Did your dad and Harriet already leave?"

"Yeah." A small laugh escaped his lips as he shook his head ruefully. "Dad was spit-shined like I've never seen him before. He'd polished his shoes and had on a crisply ironed shirt." His smile fell away. "I just hope when Harriet leaves to go back to Phoenix, he doesn't crawl back into his shell of isolation and booze."

"One day at a time," she replied, her gaze somber and telling him she might be talking about more than his father and Harriet.

Was she telling him to take their relationship one day at a time? Was she warning him not to look into the future? Not to imagine them being together forever and always?

If she was, then she was too late to warn him. His entire soul sang with his vision of their future together, and he didn't know how much longer he could hold his love inside and not speak of it to her.

"I need to get some more clothes from my place," she said, breaking into his thoughts. "Would you mind heading over there as soon as we finish our coffee?"

"Sure," he agreed easily. "What's on your agenda for today?"

"I'm not sure." She reached up and rubbed her forehead lightly with her fingertips. "Sheriff Broder is sending over another copy of the Tabitha Warren murder file later today. I think what I need to do is to go over the files of both Tabitha and Richard's murders, see if there is anything I missed."

Jerrod reached across the table and captured her hand in his. For a moment her fingers remained slack, but then they curled around his. "Johnna, you can only do your best for Erin. That's all anyone expects from you."

"My best isn't good enough unless it gets Erin an acquittal," she replied. The dark, shadowed color of her eyes showed him how absolutely important this trial had become to her.

"Johnna, you don't have to prove anything to anyone," he said as he tightened his fingers on hers.

"But I do," she protested, and untangled her hand from his. She stood and walked over to the sink, drank the last of her coffee, then rinsed out her cup.

When she turned back to Jerrod, her eyes were even darker in hue. "I have to prove something to myself. I need to shut up my father's voice in my head, and the only way to do that is to win this case."

Jerrod eyed her curiously. "What do you mean, your father's voice in your head?"

"The one that says I'm not worth anything, that I'll never amount to anything." She waved her hands and shook her head. "Never mind. Don't pay any attention to me. I'm just having a bad morning. Are you ready to go across the street with me?''

"Yeah, sure." He rose from the table, his thoughts lingering on the words she'd just spoken. He'd like to talk about the fact that Johnna's father had left her with as much emotional baggage as the trailer park had left Erin. But it was obvious from her body language that she didn't want to discuss further any of that.

As they stepped out of Jerrod's front door, Luke was just getting out of his pickup, a six-pack of beer in one hand and his toolbox in the other.

"Morning," he greeted them. "Gonna be a hot one today."

"As if it's ever anything else in Inferno," Johnna replied.

"Yeah, but the weather guys are saying it's going to be close to 120 degrees today," Luke said. He looked at Jerrod. "I'm hoping I can get the porch finished by noon, then move inside and start on those bookcases you want in the living room."

"Even if you aren't finished with the porch by noon, go ahead and move inside. I don't want you trying to work in that kind of heat," Jerrod said.

"Fine by me," Luke replied, and set his toolbox down on the half-finished porch.

"I worry about him," Johnna said softly as they walked across the street and out of earshot. "I used to worry about Mark. Mark was always so quiet and always seemed sad, then he met April. It's wonderful to see the two of them so happy together."

"What about Matthew? Do you worry about him?" Jerrod asked as they reached her front door and she pulled her key from her pocket.

"No, Matthew is too mean to worry about." She unlocked the door and they stepped inside.

"You know who I worry about? I worry about you," Jerrod said.

"You mean because of the creep who's after me?"

"Not necessarily," he countered. He shoved his hands in his jeans pockets, afraid that if he didn't do something with them, they'd reach out for her.

"I worry because you work too hard and because you need to be the best at everything you do. I worry because you hear your father's voice in your head, chipping away at your self-worth."

"I told you not to pay any attention to that," she said. "My father is dead." She raised her chin in a show of defiance. "And I know what my worth is."

Jerrod hid a smile, knowing she had no idea that her burst of bravado merely made her look younger and more vulnerable than ever. "I still worry about you," he said softly.

Her chin lowered and she cast him a smile that lit him up like a Christmas tree. When she looked at him like that, all he could think of was capturing her tantalizing lips with his and wrapping his body around hers.

"I'll just go get my things," she murmured as if she'd felt the feverish heat that suddenly radiated from him. She turned on her heels and disappeared down the hallway.

Jerrod followed her, watching the wiggle of hips that seemed to be intentionally teasing him. He shoved his hands deeper into his pockets, his fingers tingling with the need to touch her.

Once they were in her bedroom, Jerrod sat on the side of the bed and watched while she pulled clothes from the closet. She carefully laid the clothes on a nearby chair, then pulled open one of the drawers of her dresser.

The drawer contained an explosion of lacy, frilly lingerie, and flames licked the inside of Jerrod's veins. He didn't realize he'd even gotten up from the bed until he was standing just behind her.

"Johnna." Her name fell from his lips like a prayer.

She turned to face him, her lips already parted, as if she'd anticipated him and welcomed him. He pulled her into his arms and she pressed against him, as if the hunger that burned inside him was also present in her.

Her tongue met his, flickering to take the kiss as deep as possible. At the same time her hands wound tightly around his neck.

It wasn't just his body that responded to her. His heart filled his chest, and his soul felt a completeness as their kiss continued, deep and hot.

He wanted her, but didn't want to take any more than she was willing to offer. But it was Johnna who moved them toward the bed, her hands coming loose from his neck and, instead, working to unfasten the buttons of her blouse.

That was all the encouragement Jerrod needed. He gently pushed her hands away and took over the task of undressing her. He didn't say a word, afraid that anything spoken aloud would break the sensual spell that had been cast over them.

When he had her blouse unbuttoned, he slid the material off her silky skin, then pulled his T-shirt over his head. He moved his fingers to the waistband of her jeans, felt her tremor as he unzipped them and worked the denim down her thighs.

She kicked them off and in mere seconds they were both naked and on the bed.

He could feel her heartbeat pounding frantically against his own racing heart. Her skin was like velvet against his, warm, inviting velvet.

As his mouth sought hers once again, he knew with certainty that she wasn't merely a physical temptation he had to fight.

She was his destiny, the place where he needed to be.

As they kissed, his hands caressed her all over, pausing to cup her full breasts. Her nipples stiffened at the contact, and a tiny gasp escaped her as he broke the kiss and dipped his head to taste one of the buds.

Her hands stroked down his back as she parted her thighs to allow him between. He moved there, not entering her, but merely reveling in the warmth of their bodies touching so intimately.

She called his name urgently, letting him know of her incredible need for him, a need that burned inside him, as well. He entered her and looked deeply into her eyes as her moist warmth surrounded him.

There, in the smoke-gray of her eyes, he saw the same emotions he'd seen years before when they'd been nothing more than kids and crazy in love. Passion, tenderness, love—all shone from her eyes, naked and intense.

Then she closed her eyes, but he didn't feel closed out. Rather, he shut his own eyes and felt their spirits soar, then connect in an overwhelming bond of love.

They made love slowly, savoring every minute, every second of their union. Jerrod loved her with every fiber of his being, every piece of his soul, wanting her to need him as much as he needed her, wanting her to love him as much as he loved her.

They reached the height of pleasure together and, clinging to one another, descended slowly back to earth. He rolled to the side of her, but kept his arms wound tightly around her, waiting for his breathing to return to normal so he could tell her the emotions that begged to be released.

His gaze lingered on her, loving the flush that colored her cheeks, the small smile that curved her lips upward. Her eyes shone with a richness and depth that convinced him that the moment was right.

"Johnna," he said softly.

Her smile broadened. "Jerrod," she replied.

"I love the way my name sounds when you say it," he said. "And I love you." She tensed against him, but he held her close. "Just listen to me, Johnna. I can't keep it in any longer. I love you. I've never stopped loving you. You have been in my heart for so long I don't know how to stop loving you."

He smiled at her and stroked a strand of her short dark hair off her forehead. "The way I see it, loving you is a wonderful affliction that is probably going to be with me the rest of my life, and there's only one logical step to take. Marry me, Johnna. Marry me and be my wife. Share my life with me, share my dreams."

He wasn't sure what he expected, but it wasn't the frown that creased her forehead or the shadows that suddenly usurped the shine of her eyes.

He hurriedly continued, "I know your life is a little crazy right now with Erin's trial and the time you have to spend at the ranch, but I can be the part that isn't crazy."

Each of his words only seemed to make her frown deepen. "Johnna, I can't go back and erase that night with Erin. If I could, I would, but I can't. I can only live with the regret of what I did...and what I lost on that night."

"It's not that, Jerrod." She pushed against him and he released his hold on her, sitting up as she did the same. "I understand what happened between you and Erin that night."

"And you've found it in your heart to forgive me?" His heartbeat pounded in his ears as he waited for her answer.

"There's nothing to forgive. I realize now you didn't betray me."

The words should have sent relief through him, but they were uttered with such flatness that they produced an edge of anxiety inside him.

"Then marry me, Johnna. I know you love me."

"I do love you, Jerrod." She placed a hand on his face and held his gaze for a long moment. What he wanted to see in her eyes was joy, but what he saw, instead, was pain.

"Johnna?"

"Let's get dressed." She slid off the bed and grabbed her clothes. "I need to talk to you, but I don't want to talk in here."

Confused and disquieted, he dressed as she did, wondering what she could have to say to him that would bring such dark shadows to her eyes.

She'd already told him she loved him. What more was there for him to know?

When they were once again dressed, he followed her into the living room, his heart pounding a new rhythm—one of anxiety.

"Johnna, what is it?" he asked as she sat on the sofa and eyed him soberly.

For a long moment she stared off into space, the shadows in her eyes appearing to grow darker, larger. "When I left Inferno years ago to go to Phoenix, I left with a little secret."

"A secret? What are you talking about?" She was as shut down, as closed off as he'd ever seen her. He fought off a shiver of apprehension, a premonition of doom. Had they come this far only to miss their shot at happiness yet again?

"When I left here, I was pregnant—pregnant with your baby."

Jerrod gasped. She couldn't have shocked him more had she jabbed him with a cattle prod. He stared at her, utterly stunned by her words. Pregnant? She'd been pregnant? "I... Where...?" He couldn't even form a rational question as his head spun. A baby. She'd had his baby?

"I was in Phoenix, all alone and scared. And when I found out I was pregnant, I didn't know what to do. I couldn't go home, I knew what my father's reaction would be."

Her voice was cool, detached, as if she was telling a story about somebody she didn't personally know. She refused to meet his gaze, but instead, stared at the floor at his feet.

"So I worked and went to school. It was a horrible pregnancy. I was sick the whole time. One night I was so tired and so sick that I wished I wasn't pregnant anymore. And the next day I went into labor and Miranda—that's what I named her— was born...way too early. She lived for three days and then she died."

She looked at him then, her chin raised as if in defiance. A black hole of grief seemed to open up and swallow him whole. He reeled beneath the despair of not only her news, but also her cold, emotionless delivery of the facts. A baby. She'd had his baby. A little girl named Miranda. And the baby had died.

She had shared none of it with him. Why hadn't she contacted him when she first discovered she was pregnant? Why hadn't she told him all this when he had first returned to town?

Anger battled with the dark despair, and he suddenly needed to get away—away from her, away to think, away to mourn.

She stared at him with dark, soulless eyes and he wondered if somehow she'd orchestrated this moment, if she'd saved this information to share with him until it could hurt the most.

Perhaps she'd never forgiven him for his night of betrayal with Erin. Maybe waiting to tell him about Miranda until this moment, with his words of love for her still burning on his lips, was her way of paying him back.

"I...I need some time," he said as he stumbled toward the front door. "I need to think. We'll talk later."

"Sure," she replied as if she didn't believe they would ever talk again.

He turned, half-blinded by emotion, and left her house. Luke sat on his front porch, sipping a beer, but Jerrod didn't speak to him. He got into his car and pulled out, needing to drive somewhere, somewhere he could think.

A baby. His baby had lived and died, and he had to figure out why Johnna hadn't told him before now—and how God could let such a thing like this happen.

Chapter 14

Hot tears slid down Johnna's cheeks as she stared at the front door through which Jerrod had just left. She'd known he'd leave. She'd always known that once he heard the truth, he would hate her.

She'd never really believed in her heart that they would have a second chance at happiness. She'd always known she and Jerrod were doomed.

She closed her eyes and remembered those days so long ago. She'd been heartbroken, pregnant, working part-time and going to school and suffering morning sickness every hour of the day.

The days had seemed endless, her loneliness too difficult to bear. The misery of her pregnancy made everything seem that much more difficult.

She'd come home early from her job as a waitress, exhausted and sick, and for just a moment, a moment of weakness and self-pity, she'd wished she wasn't pregnant.

The next day she awoke to labor pains. It had been too early—far too early. Miranda had been born three months premature, too little and too sick to survive. Johnna had known it was all her fault.

Sobs replaced the hot tears, and she curled up in a fetal position, unsure if the pain that racked her was the memory of the loss of Miranda or the fresh, new pain of the loss of Jerrod's love.

She'd never really believed that she would be granted the love of a good man and a future of happiness. Besides, what did she know about being a wife or a mother? Her own mother had died giving birth to Johnna, and Adam Delaney certainly hadn't taught her anything about normal family life.

She hadn't been good enough to earn her father's love. She hadn't been smart enough to see beyond the obvious on the night Jerrod had been with Erin, and she'd lost her baby because deep inside she knew God didn't think she was good enough to be a mother.

The sobs came from the very depth of her, years of sorrow, years of pain bubbling up and spilling over, ripping tears from her soul.

She didn't know how long she cried. It felt like forever. When the tears were gone, the dry sobs continued, tearing through her with savage pain.

Finally the dry sobs were gone, as well, and she was left with nothing but emptiness. And the emptiness felt normal, for it was how she had felt for a very long time.

Jerrod had momentarily banished the empty feelings, had momentarily made her feel loved and cherished. He'd given her a tiny ray of hope, hope that perhaps they could find happiness together, but it had been false hope.

And she'd been a fool to believe in it even for one shining moment.

Uncurling from her position on the sofa, she sat up and wiped her eyes. It was over. It was done. She couldn't think about it anymore. It hurt too much.

It was time to draw on the strength she'd used as a child, time to isolate her emotions and shove them away deep inside her where they couldn't hurt her.

She had a woman depending on her to keep her out of prison. There was work to be done, and she had always been able to successfully bury herself in her work.

However, her briefcase was at Jerrod's house, and at the moment she didn't want to go there. In fact, later today, when she felt more mentally and physically strong, she would move her things out of his place and back here where she belonged. Alone. Where she'd always belonged.

Besides, Jerrod wouldn't want to look at her. He wouldn't want her staying at his house. Not now. Not since he knew she had wished their baby away and Miranda had died.

But she couldn't think about that anymore. If she

did, she'd lose herself to utter despair and hopelessness. She left the living room and walked into her office, forcing her mind away from Jerrod, away from the fact that her body still tingled from their lovemaking and his scent still clung to her skin.

Sitting at her desk, she dug through the paperwork on top of the desk and found an old set of notes she'd taken on the Kramer case. All she had left was her work, and it was more important than ever that she successfully defend Erin.

She'd never been a daughter, and she'd never really been a sister. She would never, ever be a wife or mother. All she could hope to be was the best damned lawyer the town of Inferno had ever seen. And that meant she had to defend Erin and win.

Time passed slowly as she read and reread what she had before her. She closed her eyes and tried to think back over all the information that had been contained in the file of the Tabitha Warren murder. There had to be a connection, some common thread, but what?

Something niggled at her, something that seemed important, but she couldn't quite put her finger on it, didn't know what it was.

Jerrod.

Jerrod.

Every time she closed her eyes and relaxed for just a moment, the vision of his handsome face filled her head, the warmth of their lovemaking flushed through her veins, and the thought of his marriage proposal filled her soul.

No more lovemaking with Jerrod. Wedding bells would never ring for them. She knew from now on she would only see scorn in his eyes, anger on his face.

The sound of her doorbell chiming preempted any tears that might have resurfaced. She left the office and went into the living room. Looking out the window, she didn't see any car, but she did see Sam Clegg on her doorstep, a file in his hand.

"Sam," she greeted him as she opened her door.

"Hi, Johnna." He stepped past her and into the living room. "I brought over a copy of that file you wanted from Sheriff Broder."

"Thanks, I appreciate it, Sam."

He dropped the file on the coffee table, but seemed to be in no hurry to leave. "How's the case coming? You go to trial in two weeks, right?"

"Right." Johnna sat down on the sofa and picked up the file, trying to look preoccupied. She didn't have the energy to make social small talk.

"You've sure been doing a lot of digging into things. I had a feeling you wouldn't be content to let sleeping dogs lie."

Johnna's gaze shot from the file in her hand to the pale-eyed deputy before her. An icy chill wound up her spine as she realized what had been niggling at her.

In both murders Sam Clegg had been the first officer on the scene. And when her car had been forced off the road, it had been Sam who had found her. Sam. Always Sam. He was the common denominator.

"You, Sam?" she asked as he placed a hand on his gun.

"You probably would have figured it out before the trial with all your questions and digging around." He drew his gun and pointed it at her. "I finally got the opportunity to get rid of that leech Richard, and now you're threatening to ruin it all."

"You killed Richard and you killed Tabitha Warren!" Johnna exclaimed, and with a new chill gripping her, realized the danger she was in.

"That's right. She was nothing but a whoring drunk. I paid her rent. I paid her bills. I thought we had an understanding of sorts. But that night she picked up some drifter in the bar and took him home with her. When I got there that night, she still had the smell of that other man on her and I hit her with my nightstick."

Johnna's gaze flickered to the thick stick that hung from his belt. "And you beat her to death." Her mouth was achingly dry as she thought of Tabitha Warren's final moments.

"Once I started hitting her, I just couldn't stop."

"And Richard Kramer somehow found out what you had done," Johnna said.

He nodded. "Richard and I went drinking one night and I got soused and talked too much. He started blackmailing me. That night when I walked into the Kramer residence and Erin was out cold on the floor, I saw my chance to get rid of the bloodsucking bastard. He was too drunk to see what was coming. And everything would have been fine if you'd just left things alone."

"You would have just let Erin go to prison for a crime she didn't commit?"

Sam's eyes flared with the first indication of anger. "Erin McCall is trailer trash just like her mother before her. The town would be better off without her in it."

"So it was you who spray-painted my car and broke into my house and warned me off the case. But why? If I didn't take Erin's case, another lawyer would." Although Johnna knew she was in danger, she needed answers and she needed time—time to figure out how to get out of this alive.

"No other lawyer in Inferno. Hell, you're the only defense attorney in town. Erin would have had to go to Phoenix or another big city to get an attorney, and they wouldn't have bothered digging into Tabitha's death, a decade-old murder."

Both Sam and Johnna jumped as her front door opened and Luke stepped in, slamming the door behind him. "Hey, what's up?"

"Luke! Run!" Johnna yelled, and jumped up from the sofa.

"Huh?" It was obvious from the slight glaze to Luke's eyes that he'd had a few beers. Before he could respond to Johnna's warning, Sam grabbed his nightstick and slammed Luke over the head.

Johnna screamed as her brother slumped to the floor. "Sit down and shut up," Sam shouted, his gun cocked and pointed at her and the nightstick raised menacingly above her.

Johnna sank back down, terror making it impossible for her to do anything but obey. Luke lay unmoving on the floor, and she couldn't tell by his position if he was breathing or not. Don't be dead, Luke, she prayed. Please, please don't let him be dead.

"Sam, please, this is crazy. Luke needs help." She hated the pleading in her voice, but would have crawled on her hands and knees in order to get her brother help.

"There's no help for Luke, and there's no help for you." He lowered the nightstick but kept the gun aimed at her. "Dammit, Johnna, why didn't you take my warnings and leave it all alone?" He stared at her for a long moment, then shrugged. "I thought for sure the car accident would have made you drop everything."

"So you stole the truck and rammed me. Why didn't you just kill me? I was unconscious. You could have ended it all right then and there."

Sam frowned. "I didn't want to kill you, Johnna. I just wanted you to leave things alone. It doesn't matter now. I can't let you go."

"If you kill me, do you really think the investigation into Richard's death and Tabitha's death is going to stop?"

"I'm not going to kill you, Johnna. You and your brother here are going to be victims of a tragic house fire. Hell, you know how slow the Inferno Fire Department is in responding to calls. Everyone's always said it's criminal that they rarely get to a fire before the building's destroyed."

He put his nightstick back in its holder on his belt, then gestured her into a straight-backed chair next to the sofa. He'd come prepared with rope in a small pouch.

He tied Johnna's hands together, then tied her ankles to the legs of the chair, then tied the upper portion of her body to the chair. With each knot he fastened her terror grew more profound.

"You'll never get away with this," she said just before he slapped a piece of tape over her mouth.

She watched in horror as he dragged Luke's body away from the front door and into the center of the living room. Luke didn't move, didn't make a sound, and she wondered if it was already too late for him.

"The fire started in the kitchen," Sam said. "Probably faulty wiring." He looked at her, his eyes in torment. "It's nothing personal, Johnna. I didn't want to have to do this. I didn't want to have to do any of it."

He closed the blinds in the living room, then disappeared into the kitchen, and Johnna heard the sound of liquid being splashed around. A moment later the distinctive odor of gasoline filled her nose. She heard a whoosh, the crackle of flames, then the slam of the back door.

She was alone in a burning house with her unconscious, maybe dead brother at her feet. Frantically she tried to get her hands loose from the rope that bound them. At the same time she contorted her mouth, attempting to dislodge the tape that covered it.

Black smoke had begun to appear in the room, a darkening haze she could taste in the back of her throat. If she didn't get free within minutes, the smoke would overcome her, and Sam would accomplish his goal—she and Luke would die in the fire.

She screamed against the tape and struggled against the binding rope. Jerrod! Her mind cried his name and she wished she could have just one more opportunity to tell him she loved him before she died. She wished she had the time to tell him how sorry she was—about Miranda, about everything.

Jerrod sat on the rock where he and Erin had once shared so many youthful discussions. He was filled with a million different emotions.

Initially, when he'd left Johnna's place, the overriding emotion had been anger. Anger that she hadn't contacted him years ago when she'd first discovered she was pregnant, angry that she hadn't told him about the baby the first day he'd returned to Inferno.

For just a moment he'd believed she'd used the information as a club of retribution, making him fall in love with her, then slamming him in the chest at the time it hurt him most.

But this thought was only fleeting. He knew Johnna better than that. She had a hot temper and she could be as stubborn as anyone, but she wasn't vengeful.

He closed his eyes and raised his face toward the hot sun. A little girl named Miranda. Grief tore through him, a grief that ripped at his very soul and forced tears to his eyes.

He hadn't gotten a chance to see her. He'd never gotten the opportunity to hold her, to tell her he loved her. She was lost to him forever, and he didn't even have a memory of her sweet little face in his head.

He'd always wanted children. Years ago he and Johnna had dreamed of a houseful of kids. They'd talked of what kind of parents they wanted to be— loving, involved parents like neither of them had had while growing up.

She'd been so cold, so matter-of-fact as she'd told him about the baby. He replayed her words in his mind, and he realized suddenly that the grief that ripped through him was not so much for the child lost, but for the woman—for Johnna.

How frightened she must have been when she'd learned of her pregnancy. How alone she must have felt. Certainly going home to her father wasn't an option.

And why would she have tried to find him? He'd betrayed her trust. He'd been the one person she'd thought she could depend on, and he'd let her down. And when she'd cast him out of her life, instead of standing his ground and fighting for their love, he'd tucked his tail between his legs and run.

He knew her well enough to know that her toneless, emotionless recitation of the facts hid enormous pain…and guilt.

She honestly believed that in that tired, frightened moment she wished the baby away, she had effectively killed the baby.

He lowered his head and said a silent prayer, asking God to kiss his baby girl for him. He wiped his cheeks, then jumped off the rock and headed back to his car.

He'd believed his mission here in Inferno was to get Johnna to forgive him. He realized now that his mission was to get her to forgive herself. And the way to do that was to love her.

He climbed into his car and headed away from the trailer park, a sudden, urgent need filling him. The need for Johnna. The need to look her in the eye and tell her that he loved her, that he would always love her.

They could mourn the loss of their baby together, the way it should have been from the very beginning. And they would build a future that would include other children and laughter and love.

As he drove back to town, his need to talk to her, hold her, was overwhelming. He had to make her understand that the death of the baby was not her fault, that God didn't work that way. Most importantly, he had to silence her father's voice in her head, the one that told her she didn't deserve happiness.

He pulled into her driveway and raced to her front

door. He turned the knob, surprised to discover it was locked. "Johnna," he yelled through the door as he knocked, "let me in. We need to talk."

He knew she was here, knew instinctively that she wouldn't have gone back across the street to his place. Besides, her car was still in the driveway.

Knocking again, he was vaguely aware of the smell of smoke. Somebody burning trash? "Come on, Johnna. Please open the door."

He thought he heard something like a muffled cry coming from inside. Suddenly he remembered the reason Johnna had been staying at his home—somebody had threatened her.

Somebody wanted to hurt her. The murderer had been after her. And he'd left her here all alone and vulnerable. "Johnna," he yelled, and realized the acrid smell of smoke was growing stronger.

He left the front door and moved to the window, but the blinds were pulled tight and he couldn't see inside. He stepped back from the house and looked up. Horror filled him as he saw a black plume of smoke spiraling upward. It was coming from the back of Johnna's house.

He needed to get inside! He glanced at his own house, where Luke's truck was parked, but the man was nowhere in sight.

"Luke! Dad!" Jerrod yelled as he ran across the street. Mack appeared at the front door. "Call the fire department," he said to his father as he picked up a hammer. "Johnna's house is on fire."

Mack disappeared inside the house and Jerrod

raced back across the street. The flames devouring the back of Johnna's house were now visible, and smoke not only swirled upward, but darkened the air in the immediate vicinity of her house.

He had to get inside. And when he did, he prayed that Johnna wasn't there, wasn't in danger. Aware that the fastest way in was through the front window, Jerrod slammed the hammer against the glass.

As the glass shattered and fell away, he looked into the living room and his heart nearly stopped. "Johnna!" he cried.

Johnna was tied to a chair, eyes closed and her head slumped to one side. Nearby Luke was sprawled on the floor. He wasn't moving, either.

Jerrod smashed away the rest of the glass and climbed into the living room, where flames had begun to dance up the wall between the kitchen and living room.

He didn't attempt to untie her, but instead, picked up the whole chair and carried it to the locked front door. He unlocked the door and flung it open, then carried her outside.

He wanted to linger over her, needing to know that she was okay, but he couldn't, knowing Luke was still inside the burning house. Regretfully Jerrod left her on the lawn and raced back inside.

The smoke was now thick and as Jerrod grabbed hold of Luke, he was overcome with a fit of coughing. He had to get Luke out of here. The heat in the room was intense, and Jerrod knew the smoke would kill them long before the flames devoured them.

Luke was a big man and a dead weight. Jerrod grabbed him under the arms and attempted to drag him to the door. But he was too heavy and Jerrod was choking, tears streaming down his face. He felt as if each breath seared his lungs, and he wondered if he was trying to save a dead man.

Suddenly somebody else was at his side. Mack McCain touched his son's shoulder and gestured that he would pick up Luke's feet. Together the two men managed to get Luke out of the house.

By this time a crowd had gathered on the lawn and Inferno's single ambulance had arrived along with a fire engine. The chair Johnna had been tied to was now empty, and somebody told him she'd already been loaded into the back of the ambulance.

As two men loaded Luke inside, Jerrod peeked into the back and saw a paramedic performing CPR on Johnna. If they were doing CPR, it meant Johnna wasn't breathing. And if she wasn't breathing, that meant that she was—

"No!" The single-word protest tore from the depths of his soul. He couldn't lose her now. Surely God wouldn't be so cruel as to take her from him now.

Frantic, he raced to his car and followed the ambulance that had just pulled away, its siren screaming the death of dreams, the demise of hope.

Chapter 15

A voice. It was a deep, smooth, familiar voice that pierced the veil of darkness she'd been under. The voice was saying beautiful things. She thought it might belong to an angel.

Funny, she'd never believed she'd get to heaven. She'd always believed she probably had a one-way ticket for the other direction.

"Don't take her from me, God. I need her in my life. She's my heart and my soul. We need a chance to get it right, to build a future together. I beg you, God, spare her. Let me have a chance to show her how valuable she is. Give me an opportunity to share with her the wonder of your love…and mine."

It wasn't an angel's voice at all, she realized. It was Jerrod's. With effort, she opened her eyes, at the same time realizing that one of her hands was tightly held by his. He sat in a chair next to her hospital bed, but he leaned forward with his head on the bed next to her side.

"I need her in my life, God," he continued. "She is my soul mate, the very heart of me. Please give me a chance to show her how much she is loved."

His words found each and every dark corner in Johnna's soul and lit them with a miraculous glow. He loved her. Even though she had confessed to him her deepest, darkest secret, the secret of Miranda. He loved her. She could feel his love emanating from him, flowing through the grip of his hand on hers.

He loved her and she loved him. And suddenly nothing in their past had the power to destroy what was in their hearts. For the first time in her life, she reached out for his love, no longer afraid, no longer feeling as if she didn't deserve happiness.

"Dear God—" Jerrod began again.

"That's the problem with preachers. They all seem to love the sound of their own voice," she said.

Jerrod's head shot up and his blue eyes, red-rimmed from tears, had never looked as beautiful. "Johnna," he breathed softly, his voice trembling with obvious relief.

"I thought you were an angel," she said as her fingers squeezed his. "I thought...I thought I was dead." Suddenly all the events that had brought her to this place in time raced through her head.

"Luke!" she cried, remembering her brother's lifeless body.

"He's okay. He's in a room down the hall. He's got a concussion, but he'll be just fine."

"It was Sam, Jerrod. Sam Clegg. You've got to tell Sheriff Broder that Sam killed Tabitha and Richard." She struggled to sit up.

"Shh." Jerrod touched a finger to her lips and pressed her back against the pillow. "Sam Clegg is already in jail. Apparently when they were taking you from your house to the hospital, you were slipping in and out of consciousness and managed to tell one of the paramedics that Sam tried to kill you. Broder went over to Sam's, and Sam fell apart, confessed to everything."

Johnna closed her eyes, for a moment remembering how close she'd come to feeling death's cold kiss. But before the chill of memory could embrace her, Jerrod pulled her up and surrounded her with his warm, loving arms.

"I love you, my sweet, beautiful Johnna," he whispered. "I feel as if I have loved you all my life and can't imagine any future without you in it."

"Jerrod." She gently pushed against him and leaned back, needing to see his face, needing to look into his eyes. "About Miranda..." Even saying the name filled Johnna with pain.

"I wish I had been there," he murmured tenderly. "I wish I had been there to share your pain, to share in the tragedy of the loss of our daughter."

She looked for anger, for blame, but saw neither in the depths of his impossibly clear, blue eyes. "Miranda's premature birth and death were horrible, but bad things happen to good people all the time. It's not a reflection of God's judgment.''

He sighed and stroked a finger down her cheek. ''Johnna, I can't take away the years your father abused you. I can't snap my fingers and erase the feelings of worthlessness he instilled in you. But I *can* spend every day of the rest of my life telling you how valuable you are and how very much I love you.''

She closed her eyes, overwhelmed by the knowledge that they were going to get a chance to right their wrongs, a second chance to love each other, and this time they would get it right.

''Marry me, Johnna. Marry me and be my wife.''

''Yes, oh, yes, Jerrod.''

His mouth took hers in a sweet kiss of tenderness, of compassion, a kiss filled with infinite promise.

''I guess she's feeling better,'' Harriet's voice rang out from the doorway.

Reluctantly the kiss was broken and Johnna was surprised to see not only Harriet, but Mack and Erin entering her room, as well.

''Oh, Johnna, thank goodness you're okay!'' Erin exclaimed as she reached the side of Johnna's bed. She grabbed Johnna's hand. ''I don't know how to thank you for all you've done.''

''You don't have to thank me,'' Johnna replied. ''I was just doing my job.''

''No...no it was more than that.'' Erin's eyes shone. ''You believed in me. You believed in my innocence.''

"Chet Maxwell has already called to say he's dropping all the charges against Erin," Harriet explained.

"Then you're a free woman," Johnna said, and smiled at Erin. "So what are your plans?"

Erin looked at Harriet, then back to Johnna. "I'm leaving Inferno. I need a fresh start in a new place. Harriet has offered me the use of her place in Phoenix for a while."

Johnna raised an eyebrow and looked at her friend. She, more than anyone else, knew how much Harriet valued her privacy. It was one of the reasons Harriet had refused to stay with Johnna here in Inferno.

"I've decided to spend a little more time here in your town," Harriet said. "So I've asked Erin to do some house-sitting for me in Phoenix."

Although Harriet carefully kept her gaze away from Mack, it was obvious what was keeping her here in town. Amazing, Johnna thought, the prim and proper law professor and the town's reformed alcoholic.

Mack shuffled his feet and stuck his hands in his pockets as a flush colored his cheeks.

"And what about you, my dear?" Harriet asked briskly. "Whatever are you going to do now that your big murder case is solved?"

"Personally, I'm hoping she's going to take some time off," Jerrod said as he once again reached for her hand. He smiled first at Johnna, then at the rest of the people in the room. "Right before you all arrived, Johnna agreed to marry me."

Jerrod's words were followed by a flurry of congratulations. Even Mack leaned down and hugged Johnna. "Take care of my boy," he whispered in her ear.

Moments later Jerrod hustled everyone out of the room, insisting that Johnna needed to rest. When they had all left, he returned to Johnna's side and gathered her into his arms.

"Now where were we before we were so rudely interrupted?" he asked.

"I think we were doing this." She leaned into him and pressed her mouth to his. His lips plied hers with hungry heat, and the loneliness and isolation Johnna had felt since her early childhood melted away.

Somebody cleared his voice from the doorway. Once again Johnna and Jerrod broke their kiss prematurely. Her eldest brother stood just inside the doorway, looking extremely uncomfortable.

"Matthew," Johnna said in surprise.

"Hi. I heard what happened. I just checked in with Luke," he said.

"And he's doing okay?" Johnna asked.

Matthew nodded. "He's got a headache and is telling everyone he will never have a drink again." Matthew shifted from one foot to the other. "I just wanted to stop by and make sure you were okay, too," he said. "I spoke to Dr. Howerton and he said he's releasing you."

Johnna looked at her brother, wishing he'd step into the room, wrap her in a hug and tell her he loved her. But it was obvious from his body language and the distance in his eyes that that wasn't going to happen.

Johnna realized it was possible the Delaney siblings might never get past the dysfunction left by their abusive father. But at least Matthew had come here, and at the moment, that was enough.

"Thank you, Matthew, for stopping by. It means a lot to me," she said.

A light flickered in his eyes as if her words had pleased him. "If you need anything, Johnna, you know where I am." He nodded to Jerrod, then turned and left the room.

Johnna sighed. "My father did a terrible thing to all of us," she said softly. "He instilled in us a basic mistrust of one another, encouraged us to remain separate. And now we don't seem to know how to connect."

"Give it time, Johnna," Jerrod said. He smiled. "You told me to give it time with my father, and look how he's blossoming. Your father has only been gone four months. Try to be patient."

She grinned at him. "You mean there might be help for the Delaney heirs yet?"

"If you and I could find each other again after all these years, then I'd say there's definitely hope that you and your brothers will find one another for the first time."

At that moment Dr. Howerton walked in and, after checking Johnna's vital signs, pronounced her fit to be released.

It was nearly fifteen minutes later that she got into Jerrod's car. "Nobody has mentioned anything about my house," she said as he started the engine. "Is it gone?"

Jerrod hesitated a moment, then nodded. "Pretty much so. I'm sorry, Johnna."

"It's all right. I had insurance." She buckled her seat belt, marveling at the fact that she'd pretty much lost all her worldly possessions, but it somehow didn't matter.

A month ago her house had been her haven, her escape from the world. It had been the only place she'd felt as if she truly belonged.

But now she knew where she belonged. Her home was with Jerrod and she'd finally come home.

The bride was missing and Jerrod knew exactly where to find her. He sneaked out the back door of his church and walked briskly down the sidewalk toward Inferno's courthouse.

In the lobby he got into the elevator and punched the button for the top floor. As he rode up, he thought over the past four days.

Erin Kramer had spent the four days packing personal belongings from the Kramer house and putting them in storage, then yesterday she had left Inferno for a new life in Phoenix.

Mack continued to surprise Jerrod, involving himself in the cleanup of Johnna's property, remaining sober and spending time with Harriet.

Johnna had divided her time between working at

the family ranch and organizing a fast wedding, a wedding that was due to take place in fifteen minutes.

And in the past four days Jerrod and Johnna had spent a lot of time talking about the things they hadn't talked about before. Jerrod shared with her the horror of the night of Erin's mother's death and the equal horror of feeling helpless to stop the events that had happened afterward.

Johnna shared with him the full details of her pregnancy, Miranda's premature birth and death, and together they had mourned. It had been four days of healing, of closing off the past and opening up the wondrous promise of the future.

The elevator door whooshed open, and Jerrod headed for the stairs that led to the roof of the building. The moment he stepped out onto the roof, he saw her.

A vision in white lace, she stood with her back to him, gazing out over the town of Inferno.

"Is my bride-to-be having doubts?" he asked.

She whirled around at the sound of his voice, and her face lit with a smile of happiness. "No doubts. I just thought I'd sneak up here and take a final look at this town as Johnna Delaney."

"The next time you look down from up here, you'll be Mrs. Jerrod McCain." His heart expanded in his chest at the very thought.

She smiled again. "Don't you know it's bad luck to see the bride before the ceremony?"

He walked to where she stood and pulled her into his arms. "Our bad luck is behind us. We've got nothing but clear sailing and happiness ahead of us."

Her gray eyes studied him soberly. "Is that a promise?"

"I can promise that I'll do everything in my power to make you happy and that I'll spend the rest of my life loving you."

"And I promise you the same thing," she replied.

He leaned down and touched her lips with his in a brief, soft kiss. "I feel like I've been married to you since the first night we made love after I returned here. In my heart, I think you've been my wife for the past nine years. Are you ready to make it legal? To be my wife not only in my heart, but before God?"

"Oh, Jerrod," she replied, her eyes holding the fires of love. "I've been ready forever."

They shared a kiss that spoke of healed hearts and second chances, a kiss of commitment, of passion...but most of all love.

*   *   *   *   *

*Will footloose bachelor Luke Delaney
finally be tamed by love?
Find out in*

TO WED AND PROTECT

*by Carla Cassidy—
the next installment in*
THE DELANEY HEIRS *miniseries.
Look for this unforgettable
Intimate Moments novel
in January 2002!*

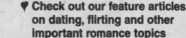

Take a walk on the dark side of love with three tales by

International Bestselling Author

MAGGIE SHAYNE

WINGS IN THE NIGHT

For centuries, loneliness has haunted them from dusk till dawn. Yet now, from out of the darkness, shines the light of eternal life...eternal love.

Discover the stories at the heart of the series...

TWILIGHT PHANTASIES
TWILIGHT MEMORIES
TWILIGHT ILLUSIONS

Available December 2001 at your favorite retail outlet.

Silhouette®

Where love comes alive™

Visit Silhouette at www.eHarlequin.com   PSWITN

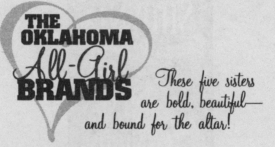